Edited by Winston Gieseke

OUT OF UNIFORM

Gay Erotic Stories

BRUNO GMÜNDER

1st edition
© 2014 Bruno Gmünder Group GmbH
Kleiststraße 23-26, D-10787 Berlin
info@brunogmuender.com

Cover design: Dolph Caesar
Cover photo: © 2014 Michael Stokes, USA
michaelstokesphoto.com
Printed in Germany

ISBN 978-3-86787-786-2

More about our books and authors:
www.brunogmuender.com

CONTENTS

INTRODUCTION
Dressed to Impress

Why do we go weak in the knees for a man in uniform? What is it about a simple outfit that can transform an ordinary guy into an object of worship? Regardless of whether he's a police officer, a military man, a firefighter, or one of those guys in sexy brown pants who delivers nice packages (both in a box and in his pants!)—there's something about the uniform makes us stop and stare.

Some say a well-fitting uniform can make a hot guy even hotter, while others posit that it's the uniform itself that's sexy. But why? Is it the fact that many uniforms—especially those representing an accomplished state, such as a military ranking or a level of law enforcement—are worn with pride, making the man stand straighter, more erect?

Does a uniform indicate strength? Does it turn a guy into a badass? Is a uniform indicative of job security? Or is it the simple fact that everyone likes a guy who can dress well? Of course, a sharp-dressed man can be a very subjective thing—I once met an interesting fellow who claimed to be turned on by anything in a *Star Trek* costume—so thankfully there are many types of uniforms for us to drool over.

Whatever your pleasure, I am pleased to present a collection of steamy tales featuring strapping studs decked out in one specialty outfit or another. Some of the stories are romantic in nature—a quest for beer leads to a fling with a soldier on leave which then helps bring an unlikely couple together in Kit Christopher's "Alameda Naval Air Station, October 16, 1969"; and a Royal Canadian Mounted Police officer searches for a wanted man but ends up wanting one in Landon Dixon's "Bear with Me"—while others deal with the uniform as an obsession. This is most glaringly true for young Corin, whose hero, a fireman, is also the object of his desire in Gregory L. Norris's "Burn"; and the relentless Will, who will do just about anything to get his handsome mailman naked in Rob Rosen's "Out of the Blue."

There's no better proof that the law of attraction works than when one sexy uniformed stud finds himself drawn to another. Such is the case in Russell Clark's "Uniformly Excited," a story about a marine going at it with a hotel bellman; and Brett Lockhard's "Officer, Interrupted," in which the fatigues of a navy SEAL just home from Afghanistan attract a baseball player fresh—or rather, hot and sweaty—from an exhilarating home game.

And believe it or not, a uniform can even lead to enlightenment. This is the theme in Joe Thompson's "What the Doctor Ordered," whose brazen young protagonist finds himself on different sides of an outfit fetish in back-to-back hookups; and in Mike Hicks's "Special Delivery," where we learn that even when a UPS guy makes an error, it can be a win-win for all parties.

But things are not always what they seem. Sometimes when the uniform comes off, the persona comes off as well: A writer who wants to blow the lid off a scout groups' antigay policy ends up blowing something else in Roger Willoughby's "Kamikaze Journo Seeks Troop Leader," while a mistreated chauffeur in 1960s' New Orleans attempts to establish some boundaries in David Aprys's "ChrisCross," and a traveler who hates airport security is surprised to find something he *does* like in Natty Soltesz's "T&SA."

Perhaps this collection's most bizarre uniform worship will be found in Mike Connor's "Into the Orange" or T. Hitman's "My Night of Wild Sex with Wilton Parmenter."

Regardless of the outfit's specifics, one thing is clear: A uniform transforms an everyday guy into a modern-day Superman, one who—ironically—we can't wait to get naked. Because the only thing sexier than a man in uniform is a man *out* of uniform.

Happy reading.

Winston Gieseke
Berlin

SPECIAL DELIVERY

Mike Hicks

There was a space right in front of the building just big enough for my car—a small miracle in that neighborhood—and I dutifully thanked the parking gods as I inched my way into the tight space. I double-checked the address before I shut off the engine, then pulled out my cell and punched in his number. He picked up on the first ring. "Yeah?"

"Joe, it's me—Mike. I'm here. I found it OK."

"Great," he said, "You wearing the uniform?"

"Yup, I've got everything. You ready for me?"

"Oh, I'm ready, buddy," he said. "Horny and ready to play." I like it when they're eager. "Come on up. It's the fourth floor, apartment six." There was the click of him hanging up. I put on the brown cap, grabbed the carton, and climbed the steps to the entrance. He buzzed me in as soon as I pressed his bell.

It was the first time I'd met him, let alone role-played with him, but I'd gotten the idea from our online chat that he'd be good at it. You can sort of tell. I started getting a boner in the elevator.

The door slid open to a dim hallway on the fourth floor. I found his door about halfway down on the left. A sound like running water came from inside. I knocked, waited thirty seconds, then pounded it hard a couple more times. The water stopped. There was some shuffling followed by the creak of footsteps coming toward the door. An impatient voice came from behind it: "Yeah?"

"Delivery." I said. "United Package Systems."

A moment passed before he spoke again. "What *kind* of package?" I'm not expecting anything."

"The package is sealed, sir." I should have said *"concealed."*

"Just leave it by the door," he said—as though he had no intention of letting me in. He was good. Little touches like that make it feel real. And hot. This was gonna be fun.

"But I'll need a signature, sir."

There was another pause. "OK, just a minute. I gotta put something on." There was the sound of further shuffling before the door swung open to reveal one of those vast, stylish loft apartments that are called studios but that are bigger than a two-bedroom house. It gave the impression of being well constructed.

So did its occupant: He stood there, a vision of pissed-off masculinity, soaking wet, ringlets of black hair clinging to his neck, naked except for the towel he held closed at the hip. There was an accent of hair on each slab of pectoral, flattened against his skin by the water. Drops ran down the hard flesh of his stomach and disappeared beneath the towel. A trail of drips led from a door at the far end of the space across the hardwood to a puddle at his feet. He hadn't mentioned his big feet—a turn-on for me—but then he hadn't mentioned how much he'd bulked up his arms and chest since that pic on the Web site was taken either.

He cleared his throat. I quickly transferred my gaze from the indented navel up to the deep brown eyes. "Um, is *that* the package?" he said.

"Yes … sorry. Here you go, sir." I handed him the cardboard cube. He took it with his free hand and examined the return address with a puzzled expression. I handed him the clipboard and pen. "Please sign by the X."

He reached for it with his other hand and the towel fell to the floor. "Sorry," he said, doing a good job of feigning embarrassment. His thick, soft dick swung left as he put the package down to pick up the towel. It looked bigger than on the Web, surprisingly bigger even flaccid. His pubes were wet and dripping. There was a trace of soapy lather on the fat head, and some suds ran from the dark meat of his ball bag down his inner thigh. I like good hygiene down there. He threw the white terrycloth back around his waist, this time securing it tightly in order to take pen and clipboard in hand. He signed and handed it back to me. "OK," he said, "thanks, buddy. Have a good night." He reached for the knob as though he really was going to shut the door on me. I took it as my cue to creatively invite myself in.

"Excuse me, Mister …" I looked at his signature and suppressed a snicker "… Mister *Dickwell*. I've been making deliveries all day, and I'm thirsty as hell. I don't suppose I could trouble you for a glass of water."

He frowned and scrutinized me for a second before responding. "Yeah, I guess so. Come on in."

I followed him across the space to the kitchen area. He opened the fridge and rooted around. There was a subtle patch of hair in the small of his back. The towel hung low enough on his ass that I could see the beginning of his crack. "I'm out of bottled water. How about a beer instead?"

"That'd be fine." I said. "I'd like that even better. He grabbed two bottles, twisted off the caps, and handed one to me. He sat down on a barstool at the counter and motioned for me to do the same before he wrapped his lips around the amber glass. We each took an initial chug.

"Thanks a lot," I said. "That really hits the spot." I spread my legs to display the erection strapped to my leg by the tight brown pants.

His eyes traveled down to the bulge, then back up to my face. Slowly a smile dawned on his face, and very slowly it turned into a knowing leer. He let the bottom of the sweating bottle touch his right nipple as he brought it to his lips for another sip. It nudged the left one on its way back down, and he let it rest there, teasing the hardening nub while we talked. "How long you been working for UPS?" he asked.

"Couple years." I took another sip and rested the butt of my own bottle on the head of the erection in my pants. It left a wet spot that made it look like my cock head was leaking. Which it was.

His smirk widened into a smile. He made no effort to hide the boner growing under his towel. He brought his beer down to rest on the tip of it, then flexed his erect cock to move the bottle up and down. "How are the benefits?"

"Oh," I said, "better some days than others—if you know what I mean." I undid the first couple buttons of my shirt. "Getting hot in here. Mind if I take this off?" I untucked it and had it open before he had a chance to answer. It slipped off my shoulders to the floor. I mouthed a silent, coy *oops*.

"Nah"—he was leering now—"can't say I mind at all. As long as you don't mind *this*." He stood and let the towel fall. He crossed his arms on his chest, leaned back, and looked down at his erection.

I gulped. It actually looked a *hell* of a lot bigger in person than on the computer screen. The head looked hard enough to burst. He wagged it back and forth a couple times and then looked up at me from under dark eyebrows. "Got any time before your next delivery, UPS guy?"

"Mike," I reminded him. I nodded and unbuckled my belt.

"Get comfortable then, Mike."

14

I was naked in five seconds. He gave me the all-over eye and seemed pleased. He pulled me toward him and put his hand on the back of my head, drawing my face to his. His tongue entered me in one violent plunge. Our pricks rubbed together and slid around in the drip while I got lost in his aggressive kiss.

I could've tongue-wrestled with him a long time, but I remembered he'd said he wanted me to be dominant, so I figured I'd go with the agreed-on plan. I put a hand on each of his plump deltoids to push him to his knees—but he resisted, driving his tongue deeper into my mouth. I pushed harder.

"No!" he growled. He took my shoulders and pushed me down. I resisted for a moment before I gave in and knelt. He was changing the script and the spontaneity of it was getting me hot. I was ready to go with it.

With his erection wagging at my eye level, he took his bottle and poured a few drops on the head. "Go ahead," he sneered, "have some beer." I wrapped my lips around the knob and sucked. The taste of beer and sweat combined with something unsurprisingly thick and salty. I popped the head in and out of my mouth in time with his groans. He took me by the hair and pulled me off it for a minute. I looked up at him. "Open wide," he said. He laid the head on my tongue and let it rest there as he poured more beer into his pubic hair. Some of it ran down his shaft and into my mouth, most of the rest went down his legs to the floor or down my chin onto my chest. I kept up my slurping until the bottle was empty.

When I'd swallowed the last drops, he grabbed the back of my head and shoved in as much of the thick shaft as I could take. I did my best. He rocked in and out of my throat a good five minutes. I was ready to let him go longer. But he stopped me and pulled me up standing.

"Come on," he said, nodding in the direction of the platform bed in the corner. I followed him to it and flopped down on my back. "Nice dick," he said.

"Thanks."

"Now turn over."

"Wha …"

"Turn over. On your hands and knees."

I hesitated. This part of the script change was less interesting to me. He didn't wait for me to comply but grabbed me by the waist and flipped me over himself, then lay down on top of me. His hard prick rested in my crack. His weight on me felt good, but I had to tell him: "Mr. Dickwell … I'm not really a bottom …"

He put his mouth next to my ear. His breath was hot. "You're about to become one—Mike, is it?" He rose and pulled my butt up in the air. "Nice," he said.

"But, really, I haven't had anyone up there in long time … I—"

"Don't worry. I'll be gentle. Mostly." He ran the tips of his fingers in circular patterns over the cheeks of my butt, moving them closer and closer to the crack, then slowly spreading it open. I heard him spit, and then felt the warm saliva run down the valley. His finger brushed my pucker and lingered, then entered me exquisitely slowly.

I relaxed into it, surprised that I wanted him to go in further. He finger-fucked me a bit, then lingered on my tight muscle ring, teasing it and playing with it, chuckling when he saw it twitch. "Clench it and relax it for me," he directed. I tried. I tightened it, then let the muscle release as best I could. Then I felt two fingers enter me. My moan resembled a whimper, but I let him continue. He leaned to my ear and whispered, "Ready for something bigger?" I'm still trying to figure out what made me say yes.

He flipped me back over on my back and stuck a pillow under my ass. His cock was wrapped in a condom he must've applied while he was fingering me. He touched my ball sac with the rubbered tip.

"Use plenty of lube, OK?" I said.

He grabbed a bottle from the nightstand and handed it to me. "You put on as much as you want." I squirted a handful onto my palm and stroked it onto the latex-sheathed bone. It surged at my touch. He closed his eyes and shuddered. "You better let me stick this in, UPS guy—before we waste a condom."

I grabbed my haunches and spread myself open. He positioned the tip against my pucker. I gave it a couple butt-kisses and then felt the pressure of him trying to go in.

"Just relax, buddy, try to push it out." I tried. He pressed. The head popped in. He started rocking before he got all the way into me, then went deeper with each stroke till he was plunging it in all the way, and pulling almost all the way out on the outstroke. With each thrust of his hips he let out a loud grunt.

My near-virginal hole couldn't take too much of that pounding, but fortunately, he was already close. He made one last brutal thrust. I let out a grunt of discomfort and he pulled out. The jism began squirting the second he ripped off the condom, and kept flowing in rhythmic spurts for thirty seconds. His sperm was steamy hot on my belly and chest. He shook the prick a few times till he was sure he'd given me every drop. I reached to stroke my own dick, but he took over for me, locking his eyes on mine and keeping me captive with them as he pulled on my shaft until I got close to that sweet place of no return. He brought his other hand to my left nipple and pinched.

The spasming started somewhere deep in my guts, then an odd and welcome clench of pleasure moved from that indistinct spot inside down to my drawn-up nut sac, intensifying till it moved up to the head of my dick. The sensation shot up the front of my body, even after the hot fountain of juice began shooting, and exited me in a low, involuntary shout. It wound down like a siren spending itself till the only sound left was my breathing and his. He decreased the pressure on my nipple but held on to my cock for a long while after I finished, even after it got soft. I reached for his. It was still erect.

He chuckled. "It stays hard for a while after I cum," he said. Some guys are just made that way, I guess. My thumb and forefinger couldn't reach all the way around it. I gave it a couple strokes. He grinned and let go of me, then got up to get the towel from where he'd dropped it, and came back to wipe our mingled semen off my belly. "Thanks," I said.

"No problem. Mama always taught me to clean up my mess." He finished the job and tossed the towel back on the floor, then lay down next to me on the bed. He kissed me, gently this time, just lips touching, tender with the tongue. I could have stayed with that kiss a long time, but reality hit me to keep from doing something I might regret. It was, after all, just an Internet hookup. Fun, but not a good idea to take it too seriously.

I got up and found the elements of my uniform. He played with the head of his boner while he watched me dress. I grabbed the box and clipboard and paused before heading for the door to get a last look at him. "You know," I said, "you should really get some new pictures."

"What do you mean?" He propped himself up on an elbow.

"New pictures—for your Web ad. You look a lot different now. Hotter, frankly."

He looked genuinely confused. "*Web ad?* I don't have ..."

We looked at each other for a few seconds of puzzled silence. "You're not roleplayslut69?"

"Um, *no*, I don't know what you're talking about."

"Isn't this 307 Fernandez, apartment six?"

"Well, it's 307 all right, but ..." He slapped himself on the forehead and rolled his eyes, then grabbed the cum-soaked towel from the floor and wrapped it back around his waist. He went to the door and cracked it, then checked to make sure no one was in the hallway

18

before opening it all the way. "Shit," he said. He touched the metal number six on the door. It was loose. He rotated it with his finger. It became a nine. "That top nail came out last week. I really did mean to fix it ..."

"So, this isn't ...?"

He shook his head. "Nope." Another pause, then: "So, I'm guessing you don't really work for UPS ..."

I shook mine. "And your last name really *is* Dickwell?"

He nodded. There was a moment of stunned silence before we fell against each other laughing, and a good several minutes before we stopped. When we'd both recovered, we hugged, and he lay back down on the bed. I put on my cap to go.

"Well, thanks for the delivery, in any case." he said.

"Yeah, and thanks for, um, opening me up to new experiences."

"No problem. If you care to make this a regular stop on your route, I might open you up a bit more." He winked.

"I'd like that. I'd better get going now, though. Where is apartment nine anyway? He must be wondering what happened to me."

"Other end of the hall, but don't you think he's probably given up on you by this point?" He locked his hands behind his head, exposing the dark patches of hair in his pits. The scent made it to my nostrils in an instant, making an electrical connection to my nuts. He was, incredibly, still hard. He wiggled it and grinned. "Why don'tcha make *his* delivery some other time?"

I thought about it for a second, then shrugged and started to unbutton my shirt again.

ALAMEDA NAVAL AIR STATION, OCTOBER 16, 1969

Kit Christopher

I was in my "tough" period at this point. I remember smoking cigarettes to look bad and drinking when I could get a hold of beer. I hung out with my older brother and his friends because they could get in much more glamorous trouble than I could with my friends. It was that awkward summer before college starts, and we were old enough to get in trouble, but not old enough to figure out how to avoid it …

My brother's friends liked me because when we went down to Webster Street to see if we could get a sailor to buy us liquor, I always fared better than they did. What they didn't know was that these gobs wanted to think they were hot stuff, so when I'd get within ten feet of a sailor I was fairly well swooning. And they loved it. Standing outside Lucky's Liquor in my little bellbottomed jeans, I'd wait till a sailor staggered by and then I'd bat my eyelashes and do my "Please, Mister …" routine. Sometimes I'd even get a lascivious comment in addition to the booze.

The night I met Buzz we were particularly well off because my brother's best friend Rick had borrowed his father's car. Well, not borrowed, exactly. Rick's father was prone to passing out after dinner. So, there were six of us riding around in the beat-up 1961 Lincoln Continental, looking to get in some big trouble.

I was hoping the other guys would disappear and Rick and I would end up alone together. I was Rick's default action. He'd graduated high school and gone to work in his dad's auto shop, and there had been plenty of nights when Rick was horny and we'd end up using his keys to open the auto shop to "hang out and drink beer." Rick would sprawl out on the red vinyl sofa in the waiting area and read a *Playboy* magazine while talking about how horny he was. Soon enough, his big ex-football-star cock would get hauled out of his jeans and, while his face was buried in Miss September's spread, I would quietly kneel on the floor in front of him. I'd stroke his thighs and sometimes pull his pants down around his ankles. He would say nothing. It never occurred to me as I was blowing him in the near dark of the waiting area that he couldn't see anything in that magazine. It was too dark. But the magazine served another purpose. It was a rotogravure wall of denial. Rick could happily let his best friend's little brother slobber his big load down if he had the security blanket of a *Playboy* in between us.

Romance in a small town is pretty scarce for a guy like me. I never even thought to expect it.

At about seven-thirty we headed down to Webster Street to score, and I could feel my pulse rise. I loved doing this for two reasons. First, because the guys made a big deal over my nerve and ability to get the sailors to buy us booze; and second, because of the fleeting and elicit contact I'd have with the sailors. I loved the conspiratorial feeling.

The *Enterprise* had arrived in town the day before. It was Friday night and the streets were swarming. We had no problem finding sailors. There were guys in clean white uniforms and guys in woolen navy blue. Then there were the guys from landlocked states, with roses in their cheeks, standing out like sore thumbs with their nearly shaved heads. It was, after all, 1969. They tried to make up for it wearing "groovy" clothes. Fringed buckskin jackets were big at this point. Tight white jeans and a skintight tie-dyed T-shirts. Maybe even some beads or a headband. I posted myself outside of Lucky's and lit a cigarette while the guys waited in the car in the Safeway parking lot across the street.

A big blue Cadillac pulled up in front of the store and the passenger door opened up. A fairly drunk sailor tumbled out, yelling at the driver, "Hey, ya fuckin' cocksucker … git yer hands off me!" He landed on his drunk, navy blue butt and the car sped away into the night. I stood and watched as the guy pulled himself together and brushed himself off.

He looked at me and laughed. "Shit, man, ya hitch a ride in this fuckin' place and they think ya owe 'em some meat or somethin." As he swaggered toward me, I saw that he wasn't so much drunk as out of control. He had an exaggerated macho strut that gave his slim hips quite a roll. His navy blue wool looked glued on, especially around his thighs and shoulders. He wasn't pretty, but he had a streetwise, seen-it-all look on his late-teenaged face that made my throat close up. And he was a big guy, about fifty pounds more than me and almost a foot taller.

I gathered myself together and began my pitch, "Excuse me, Mister, can I talk to you for a minute?" I told him to come around the side of the building and he seemed intrigued. "We need three six-packs of talls, but we don't have ID, can you help us out?" He looked at my wadded up dollar bills and smiled.

"Well, buddy, the problem is I'm only twenty and I don't got an ID either."

22

"Oh, don't worry, they always sell beer to sailors here—I know, 'cause guys get it for me all the time."

"Is this a regular hustle for you or somethin'?"

"My older brother and his friends make me do it for them," I whined slightly. I batted my eyelashes and he smiled real big this time and looked at me in a way that made me shiver, even tho' it was a warm night. He took the money and was back in a flash with the beer and a fresh pack of Marlboros. He offered me a cigarette.

"So, what you gonna do for me now, buster?" I gulped and he laughed. "Don't worry kid. Can ya git me a ride down to Park Street? I wanna go to the pizza joint there …"

With four of us jammed into the backseat of the Lincoln the sailor seemed even bigger than before—all thighs and arms. He lifted both arms up and rested them on the back of the seat behind us. I was on the door under his left armpit. He smelled like Old Spice.

Buzz, as he'd introduced himself, was smart to get to the other side of town: less competition. As we bumped along I felt his arm come to rest on my shoulders, then his fingertips on my arm. We were all drinking the beer as fast as we could and Buzz had joined us. I had a hard-on as I pretended I was his girlfriend or something. From time to time he would lean across me to look out the window and his neck would be right in my face, all pink and smooth where it went from his bleachy-smelling white T-shirt to his fresh crew cut. Each time he sat up again his fingers would get closer to my nipple and finally his hand was right on my left pec, the fingers lightly grazing back and forth over the hardened nub.

I couldn't help but squirm as he looked at me, eyes boring into mine, face soooo close, and whispered low, "Feels good, don't it?" And with that he began to really flick and twist my little nipple in earnest.

The only person in the car aware of what was going on was Rick, as he was looking at us in the rearview mirror. But I wasn't worried about Rick. I could tell he was getting a thrill out of it. Besides, I figured Rick owed me a chance to be with a guy who could admit I was in the same car with him.

We let Buzz off at Leon's Pizza & Pool and then we were off again. I saw, as we drove away, Buzz standing on the street with what seemed like a huge lump underneath those thirteen buttons. I was flushed and almost sick with excitement. I had to get back there. I told Rick to take me home. Rick smiled at me in the rearview mirror and asked why. I said I was sick. Everybody laughed except for Rick, who said that I did look pretty bad, and who needs a kid now anyway—weren't they looking to find girls?

Thank you, Rick.

I didn't even go in the house; I just got my bike out of the garage and pedaled my ass as fast as I could back to Leon's.

Leon's was interesting. My mother used to send me down there to get pizza for everyone when she didn't want to cook. It was pretty sleazy for Alameda, especially the east side. It attracted bikers and girls with heavy makeup. I used to love to go there because of the bathroom. The walls had the filthiest drawings and comments I'd ever seen. I learned a great deal about the sexual behaviors of adults from those walls. Sometimes the bikers and hoods would come in and take a piss next to me in the trough urinal. One or two would even look over and guiltily show me their hard cocks. I was way too scared to do anything there. But that didn't stop anyone from long games of show and tell. I remember one guy with a big, hard, uncut cock that could piss while it was fully hard and sticking straight up. The piss hosed up and splattered the wall above the trough and back-splashed on us both, getting our shoes wet.

So, yeah, I offered to pick up pizza for my family on my bike all the time.

24

Because they served pizza I could get in even tho' I was under twenty-one, and I have the feeling that's why Buzz went there as well.

I lit a cigarette and brushed my long shaggy hair back to try and look a little older but it all fell back into my face. I went to the counter and ordered a coke from the old woman, and she asked me what kind of pizza I wanted. No pizza, I said, and she said I had to get out—no food, no loitering for eighteen-year-olds. A big-chested burly guy with a goatee and a motorcycle cap hooked his arm under mine and said, "This way, youngin," as he took me out the front door. Shit, I hadn't even seen Buzz. I stood outside and looked in the window for him. Then I felt a tap on my shoulder.

"Hey buddy, what happened to your friends?" He stood smiling at me with a couple of bottles of beer in one hand and scratching his stomach under his uniform with the other. I smiled back. He slung his arm over my shoulder and we started off towards the bridge. "So I'm stuck with ya now, huh?"

I nodded, awestruck.

"I hope you know what yer doin', kid." I nodded in the affirmative. "We'll see about that." He winked at me.

We sat on some pilings on their sides under the Park Street Bridge and smoked and drank our beers. Small talk. He told me where he was from (Wyoming), and I told him this was where I'd had my first cigarette. He laughed and said, "Well, I hope ya still got a few firsts left 'cause I plan to get me at least a couple of them."

Buzz flicked his Marlboro into the estuary and I imagined that I could hear it hiss as it hit the water. "You're a pretty boy, prettier than my girl in Cheyenne. You don't even shave yet, do ya buster?" His hand stroked my cheeks and hair and I panicked. I suddenly realized what "first" he planned to have of mine. It was the remark about his girlfriend.

"Buzz, have you ever done it with that girl in Cheyenne?"

25

"Well, not actually, but we is gonna get married as soon as I'm out of the navy."

"Have you ever fucked anyone?"

"Hey! Whad'ya think, man, I'm in the fuckin' navy. I've been around!" We sat in silence. "Well, I got blowed a couple of times, that's it. Have ya ever blowed another guy, kid?"

"Well sort of …" I tried to sound innocent, but not so innocent as to scare him off.

"Your brother?"

"No, Rick, the guy who was driving the car—but he made me do it."

This elicited a response of sympathy; he cuddled close to me on the log we sat on and hugged me to him. "Don't worry, buster, I ain't gonna make ya do anything ya don't want." As he hugged me he felt me all over and put his hands up under my shirt to feel my chest as if I had tits. "Can I kiss ya?"

I closed my eyes and leaned my head back, waiting for the dreamy romance of my first real kiss. Buzz's fuzzy hairs on his upper lip brushed with mine as he nuzzled my face. He began in little soft kisses and soon had about a half-a-foot of tongue in my mouth and was panting like a dog. With incredibly busy hands he'd managed to get my T-shirt off and undo his thirteen buttons so that the flap was hanging down and his stalk of cut meat was sticking straight up through the vent in his navy-issue boxer shorts.

My arms were up around his shoulders so he took one down and whispered in my ear. "C'mon, kid, jerk on my cock, huh?"

I reached down and lightly glided my hand all over the big pole and then held on tight while I jerked it in short strokes behind the head. The lights from the bridge were bright enough that I could see a slag of clear goo forming at the tip of his cock and running down the underbelly, lubricating my fingers.

He stood up suddenly and cupped my head in his hands, kissing the top of it, and begged me: "Please buddy, put it in your mouth and suck on it real good for me, huh?"

Looking up at him with his white navy cap pushed forward over his plaintive eyebrows, his peach fuzz face, and the spray of freckles across his nose, I couldn't imagine anything more I wanted than to feel his big navy cock pushing into my mouth.

I leaned forward and slathered my tongue all around the head while I hauled his big testicles out from the fly in his boxers. They were smooth and shiny in the bridge lights.

"Just tell me if I hurt ya," he said as he began pushing my head down onto the meat. I gagged as it hit the back of my throat and he kept asking if I was OK, but he never stopped, and spit ran down off his balls into my hands. "Get the balls too, kid." He hefted them up to my mouth, pushing them into my lips. As I worshiped his cock, he pulled his top off and laid it on the huge piling next to me. He dropped his pants and pulled them over his shoes and I flowed with him, never losing grip on his meat. He stood me up, undid my bell-bottoms and they fell to the ground as my boner popped up. I wore no underwear, which shocked him.

"You must really be some kind of hippy kid, huh?"

Wyoming, I thought.

He laid his pants down next to the shirt, and I could see that he was planning to use his clothes to prevent me from getting splinters. Gallant. He sat down again and hugged me to him, our fully naked bodies touching everywhere. He sat me on his lap with my pants still caught around my ankles and kissed me again while his rock-hard pole poked up at my butthole. He reached between my legs and fingered my ass, not sticking it in but getting it ready to have something stuck in it. "I don't know kid, do you think you can take it back there? It feels real tight."

"Uh-huh," I said, nodding. "You just need to spit on it or something."

He brought his hand to his mouth and put a glob of spit on his fingertips, then went back to my asshole. In truth, he could have done anything he wanted to me as long as he kept kissing me like that. His tongue kept going new places I had never known about in my own mouth, and it felt like a velvet-wrapped muscle.

Aided with spit, his index finger plopped right into my ass up to the first knuckle, then, as he worked his hand in a fuck-like motion, he got his finger in to the hilt. I was panting and squirming and wondering how I could possibly handle anything more. It was a strange sensation. But when he got it far enough he rubbed what I now know to be my prostate gland. And this changed everything. And I mean *everything*. I've spent the decades since trying to find other people to help me locate it again. With much success, I might add.

As Buzz plunged his finger in and out of my newly found toy, he stood and lifted me with him so he could set me down on the carefully thought-out and prepared bed he'd made for me. His navy uniform was scratchy but not as bad as the bare piling would have been. His clothing smelled like Old Spice and cigarettes, maybe even a trace of Wildroot. My feet were still attached at the bottom by my jeans but my knees were spread wide to straddle the circumference of the log.

Buzz sat just behind my ass with his legs slung over mine and played with my buns while his dick bounced against my balls.

He was adding spit to his cock to get it into me, and I was beginning to think he was right, that it would never fit. I felt panicky and started to get up off the piling. He stopped me with one big hand on the small of my back, pinning me down on the log like a stuck butterfly. "Hey buster, relax and this'll go a lot easier."

He leaned up over me, bracing himself with one hand just to the side of my face and used his other hand to stroke his very wet cock against my very wet hole like a big meaty wand. He gently poked and stabbed at my hole in a fairly non-threatening way until I was squirming and panting as I dry-humped the log.

"Uh, Buzz, I think you can try to … well, why don't you …?"

He pushed, and the blunt head plopped in to the top of his circumcision scar. Don't ask me how I know, I just know. Anyway, I squealed, and he brought his hand to my face so fast to shut me up that it was almost as if he'd slapped me. His lips were next to my ear whispering to me, "Just relax, baby, think about how good it's gonna feel to get that whole big dick inside ya. It won't hurt for long, but ya gotta get the whole thing in first."

I squirmed forward just far enough to disengage with a fair amount of pain. I instantly regretted it. I turned over my shoulder to look at him and apologize. He kissed me sweetly on the lips and put his finger to my mouth to hush me. Then he began to kiss his way down my bare back, sometimes licking, sometimes biting. When he got to the top of my ass crack he began to slather his tongue down the crack, leaving a good deal of spit as he went.

What he did next had certainly occurred to me before, but I'd assumed I was the only one to think of something so depraved: He began to jam his tongue in and out of my hole in a very deliberate way, and it did the trick—my asshole opened up, willing and ready. He was pulling my cheeks apart with his hands while he did it.

Just as I began to groan uncontrollably—whimper, actually—he swooped over me again, putting all his body weight on me and plunging half his cock up my newly opened hole. I gasped as he began minute sawing-back-and-forth motions that would put a little more of his stalk inside me with each forward thrust. It's a technique that I, myself, have used on virgins ever since.

He did not lie. As soon as he was in to the hilt, the pain began to disappear and I surrendered to the wonderful helpless feeling of

29

being royally fucked by a big sweaty sailor. I could not have prayed for a better deflowering. Buzz whispered in my ear all the wonderful things a virgin loves to hear:

"You're the best."

"Your ass is hot and tight."

"You're the only one."

"I'll love you forever," etcetera.

Meanwhile, I writhed and twisted, trying to feel his thickness penetrate every area I could, all the while stimulating my new friend, the prostate gland. I also gasped out my own fair selection of virgin-style babblings:

"It's too big."

"Please be gentle."

"Oh my God, it feels so big and good."

And finally, "Fuck me harder, sailor."

He began to slam me into the piling now. I felt the air punched out of me with each downward thrust. The sweet nothings he whispered into my ear took a darker turn. He muttered hot and wet into my ear: "Oh fuck yeah, boy. Gonna open that hole of yours good now with my big cock. I knew you were a slut when I saw you by that liquor store, honey. I knew I'd get my cock up that pretty little hole of yours. You were fucking squirming like a little whore when I played with your nipple while your boyfriend was getting off watching us in the rearview mirror."

I felt degraded and turned on all at once.

He bit me on the ear and said, "Get up, I wanna fuck you like a girl now." Not knowing what he meant, I was a little offended but not enough to argue. He pulled my pants inside-out and off over my shoes and turned me onto my back. With my legs up over his shoulders, he had no problem working his big navy dick into my opened ass. Now we could kiss. My mouth and my ass were both very busy as he huffed and snorted on top of me. He hugged me real tight and pounded my ass while his face was pressed to the side of my neck. Three short hard pounds and he was suspended in air, and the only thing I could feel was the steady throb of his cock plugging my hole as it shot spasm after spasm of sailor jizz into my guts.

Slowly, I felt my heart stop racing as he eased out of me with a plop. I heard a train whistle from the other side of the estuary and a breeze blew up from the water, making all my skin go goosefleshed and shivery. He flopped back down on me and ground our sweaty and sticky bodies together to warm me back up. My cock was hard as stone between us and he belly-rubbed me as he hugged me so close and so tight that I swooned. He began humping me and working his big swabbie tongue back into my mouth. I was so close to cumming that I was whimpering and squealing into his mouth. He humped and rubbed my cock between us until I exploded, and each of us could feel the zing-zing-zing of my jizz shooting between our bellies.

After a couple of cigarettes, we picked our clothes up from beneath logs, beer bottles, and used rubbers. My T-shirt was kind of wet but he put his arm around me to keep me warm. We picked up two more beers as we walked down the empty streets of Alameda.

We snuck into my parents' backyard and talked and nuzzled until almost dawn. He patted my ass as I hiked up the ladder I kept near my bedroom window for late night entry. When I got to my bedroom in the front of the house I could see his cocky sailor strut as he walked down the street in the pre-dawn haze.

Then I saw the interior light of Rick's Lincoln as he quietly exited the car. He must have been there since we got home. I heard the ladder creak against my window sill and suddenly Rick was standing there in my room, huffing from climbing up the ladder.

31

"I thought that gob would never leave. So? Did he fuck you?" he whispered as he put his arms around my waist.

"What's it to you?" I murmured into his neck. I had always wanted him to hold me like this.

"Well, at first I got mad. Then I got turned on thinking about it." This was more than Rick and I had ever said about what we'd done.

"So what? Now *you* want some?"

His big hand slid down to my ass and he gently cupped my ass cheeks. I could feel a little leakage down there from Buzz's cum. Rick gently eased me back to my bead and I kind of melted under him as he crawled on top of me in my wagon wheel single bed.

Then, for the first time ever, he kissed me. Tongue and everything, and my head nearly exploded I was so happy, tuned on, blown away.

"Yeah," he said. "I want some."

UNIFORMLY EXCITED

Russell Clark

I'm a marine who, just last month, came back from my third tour of duty in Afghanistan. So, I decided I deserved a break after living the rough life of a military man for the better part of three years.

I began my transition to civilian life by giving myself a trip to sunny San Diego, where I planned to soak up some sun at one of those beautiful beaches and maybe find a few other military guys who'd like a little fun on the side—or on their backs.

Upon checking in to my hotel, I was escorted to my room by a good-looking bellman, about my age: twenty-four or so. He was as tall as me, too, at six feet, with curly black hair and a Roman nose. I've always been turned on by men in uniform (I can't tell you how many times I jerked off in the barracks thinking about guys in my unit who looked so hot in their dress blues!), so even the bellman's sharp red and black outfit gave me a chubby as we walked down the hall to my room.

I was in civilian clothes: a white polo shirt that fit as tight as I could get it, showing off my well-developed pecs, flat stomach, and muscled arms that we marines call our "guns." My khaki cargo shorts fit tight as well, making a tempting display of my hot, high-riding ass and worked-out legs. White sneakers completed the look. I looked pretty damn hot. If this bellman had a liking for men, I was sure he'd find something about me that turned him on.

He opened the door to my room, which was on the fifth floor in a corner of the hotel. There were two balconies, one facing the ocean just a hundred yards away and another facing the hotel tower across the courtyard. It was a nice room, with a huge king-sized bed and a bathroom that looked like it belonged in a day spa, all granite and white porcelain, with a Jacuzzi tub and a shower that could easily fit three or four. All four walls had mirrors, and I imagined myself stepping out of the shower in the morning, naked, tanned and appreciating my muscles in the reflections from all directions.

The bellman, whose name was Ted, turned down the corner of the bed, saying that other servicemen who'd visited the hotel had expressed appreciation for the facility's comfortable beds and soft sheets after so many months of sleeping in bunks. He then opened the closet and offered to hang up my things. I said "Sure," and he plopped my suitcase on the bed and unzipped it. I was hoping he'd see my leather harness and get the idea that I was interested in unloading more than just my suitcase. He hung up the shirts first, and then lifted out a pair of jeans and some black cotton slacks. He even opened a drawer in the dresser and placed my tight white briefs, socks, and wifebeaters inside.

The only thing left in the bottom of my suitcase was my harness. I assumed Ted would have one of two reactions: either he'd be "all business" and just hang it on a hanger, or he'd say something about it. I was hoping for the latter.

I got my wish. He picked the harness up with both hands, looked in my direction, and held it out as if he were imagining it on me. "Nice!" he said, before balancing the leather straps expertly on a wooden hanger and placing it in the closet.

It was enough of a cue for me to know Ted wasn't exactly straight and narrow—or at least not narrow.

"Would you like to try it on?" I asked.

He looked at me curiously, as if I were the first person who'd ever asked him a question. Then he shook his head quickly from side to side, as if trying to wake himself. "Oh, I think it would look much better on you, sir ..."

With that, I grabbed my shirt at the waist and lifted my arms above my head, stripping off the stretchy garment in one smooth motion. I stood before him, naked to the waist, with my dick beginning to tent the crotch of my shorts. Just the thought of dressing in leather is enough to get me hard, and now I was in a private room with only a bellboy in a sexy uniform.

Ted took the harness and its hanger out of the closet and handed it to me. "Here you are, sir." Him calling me "sir" was just good manners, but it was starting to fuel a little dom-sub fantasy for me, which turned me on even more. I took the harness off the hanger, unfastened the buckles that met in the middle of the chest, and then slipped my arms through the straps. Ted took a step closer and pulled the straps tight, buckling me in. I was fully hard now, and unabashedly reached for Ted's crotch. He was hard as steel, too.

Once the straps were securely fastened, Ted leaned down and licked at my nipples, which instantly became stiff. While his mouth was busy, he wasted no time unzipping my shorts and letting my dick loose. I was going commando, as I usually do in my MARPAT utility uniform, so there was no underwear to slow him down. He took my meat in his hands, wrapping both around the shaft like kids do on the grip of a baseball bat to see who swings first. I'm no porn star, but I'm more than respectable—and with both his hands on my cock, my head was still visible above his fist.

I went for the zipper in Ted's sexy uniform. His cock was long, thin, and uncut. I then undid the button on his waistband, and his pants quickly slid down his legs, revealing a pair of bright blue bikini briefs. Ted let out a satisfied moan. His ass was beautiful, a perfect half circle that rode high on his tightly muscled legs.

I pulled the briefs down, too, and they came to rest in a bunch around his ankles. He returned the favor and unfastened my waistband's button, allowing my shorts to drop. I kicked them off and stood in front of Ted stark naked, hard, and horny as hell.

The edge of the bed was the closest place to sit, so I seated myself there and Ted dropped to his knees before me. God, this was making me hot! Here I was, wearing just a Speedo tan line, a harness, a hard-on, and a smile, and there was a sexy bellman kneeling in front of me, about to take my dick for a ride.

Ted seemed to like what he saw: a pair of low hanging balls and my cock at attention. He went for the nuts first. He started with a few licks of my shaved sac and then suctioned first one, then both of the balls into his hot mouth. His nose was right up against the base of my shaft, and it felt amazing.

He let them fall from his mouth, then wrapped his left hand tightly around the base of the sac, stretching my balls down a couple of inches and pulling my cock forward so it pointed straight at his face. He inserted a finger in his mouth and wetted it well, then used it to trace the outline of my asshole as he slowly began circling the head of my cock with his tongue.

I've always been a top. But I know how much bottoms enjoy getting a dick inside them, so I was willing to let Ted do a little experimenting with his finger. It wasn't the first time I'd had something in my ass, but I wasn't all that experienced down there. It felt great! My cock was slowly sliding in and out of his mouth while he tugged on my nuts and fingered my ass. Sparks were flying all over my crotch as he hit every erogenous zone in the neighborhood!

36

I'd been thinking hot thoughts since first laying eyes on Ted in his uniform, so I knew I wasn't going to last long, especially not the way he was servicing me. I urged him to stand, so he let go of my cock, balls, and asshole and stood directly in front of me, his dick dangling delectably in my face. I began stroking my cock as I went down on him. He was a little longer than me, but not as thick, so deep-throating him wasn't a tough challenge. I could tell he liked it by the sounds he made, especially as I took him all the way down to the hilt and felt his pubes tickling my nose.

At this, he moaned like a wounded animal.

The next few minutes brought an avalanche of good feelings: sucking a nice, uncut cock, stroking myself to the edge, and having Ted reach down and tweak my nipples with his fingers as we rode the wave to orgasm. It happened almost simultaneously.

I erupted first, and had to back off of Ted's dick to let out the muffled cry that had built inside me. My seed splattered onto my stomach in four big gushes. Then Ted grabbed his pole and stroked himself two or three more times until he let out a geyser of cum that splashed onto my chest, dripping all over the harness.

"Wow, you really know how to make a hotel guest feel welcome," I said after a second.

Ted smiled and pulled up first his blue briefs and then his red uniform pants. He seemed eager to get back to his work. Still naked, I walked to the tricked-out bathroom for a towel and took a moment to admire my appearance in the mirrors. My hot body, the sexy harness, and the splashes of cum on my chest and stomach made for a memorable reflection—one I'd have to remember when I jerked off in that room later.

Cleaning myself off as I returned to the foot of the bed, I gave Ted a big, wet kiss that he returned with a vengeance. He was as good at kissing as he was at giving head.

"You just made my trip," I said as I placed my hand on the small of his back and walked him to the door. "Thanks."

"My pleasure, sir," he responded.

Since I was still naked as a jaybird, I opened the door and stood behind it, giving him a clear path to walk past me. He started to leave, then stopped and turned to face me. With the door wide open, he planted another kiss right on my lips, then walked away down the hall.

I was spent. I collapsed on the bed to enjoy those little aftershocks that come with a particularly satisfying orgasm. As I shuddered in ecstasy, I thought about what other "activities" I might engage in on this little vacation. I promised myself I'd have several days to pursue some erotic pastimes, so I allowed my eyes to shut and entertained several ideas about how I might get Ted to come back to my room.

Several hours later, at eighteen hundred, I came to, shocked to see that it was already twilight outside my window. I'd been expecting to go to the beach on my first day in town, and now the sun had set. Oh well, maybe a little evening stroll on the sand might work out some of the kinks I'd been carrying around since trying to sleep through mortar attacks and IED explosions.

I was still dressed—or undressed, as it were—as I'd been when Ted left my room. I noted that the curtains on the balcony facing the courtyard were still open, so I got up to close them. Directly across the open area, I saw the silhouette of a man standing on his balcony facing my room. Although it was fairly dark outside, I could tell he was shirtless and drinking a cocktail, thanks to the lights in the room behind him.

As I closed the curtains, I saw him raise his glass, as if offering me a greeting. Which meant he could see me as well as I could see him. He turned and walked back into his room, where he refilled his glass and turned on another light. Suddenly I could see him clearly: He was as naked as I was.

Maybe it was the relaxing effects of the alcohol that prompted him to return to the balcony a little bit more boldly. His cock was half-hard now, which I could easily see from my own balcony, not more than fifty feet away. I could also see that he was about six feet tall, blond, and built like a boxer. His chest was hard and sculpted, his abs just as hard and flat, and his long legs muscled and defined.

There wasn't much hair on his body, and what was there was as blond as the hair on his head. His hair was cut high and tight, in the typical military style, so I knew he was a brother in arms.

My cock, responding to this stimulus, started rising to attention again. Almost without thinking, I grabbed the striped drape and held it up, covering the lower half of my body. But the mysterious man across the courtyard shook his head. I took a quick look around to see if anyone else could see me, then stepped out onto the balcony, just as he'd done. Other rooms had a view toward mine, but they were either dark or the drapes were drawn, so it was only the two of us out there enjoying the brisk night air.

The man smiled, as if to acknowledge my bold move out into the open. He swept his hands across his chest and nodded approvingly, making reference to the harness I was still buckled into. To show how pleased he was, his cock rose to full height. He reached his hand down and slowly began stroking himself without taking his eyes off me. My own hard cock was begging for the same treatment, and I followed his lead, tugging my pulsing dick.

We were a study in contrasts: him blond, tanned, Nordic, and smooth-bodied; me shorter, stockier, Italian and hairy. I'd gotten plenty of sun in Afghanistan, but because my uniform had always covered my legs, only the top half of my body had darkened to more than my ordinarily olive complexion. That was something I hoped to rectify here at the hotel's pool or the nearby beach. His tanned skin, on the other hand, made him look incredibly hot, and his tan lines really got me going.

Even from this distance I could tell he was hung. His skin was lily white where his swimsuit usually covered him, and I marveled at the sight of his thick, uncut cock. Every few minutes, he'd take a break from stroking his porn-star sized dick to take a sip of his drink, always ending with that universally-recognized "cheers" movement of raising his glass, as if congratulating me on what I was doing. Or doing to him.

I wouldn't have thought I was that close to cumming, but after only a few moments of imitating his movements, I could feel that familiar electricity starting at the base of my dick and coursing through my body. Within the next ten seconds, I had to decide whether to get off or slow this session down.

I opted for the second choice, leaning back against the sliding glass door of the balcony, which cooled my body and took some of the starch out of my erection. I continued watching my exhibitionist friend stroke himself—he now stood with his legs spread wide and had both hands on his massive cock.

What happened next really surprised me. He removed his hands from his cock. Then, without touching himself, he came in spasms, with jizz landing everywhere: at his feet, on the balcony's railing, even flying over the top of the wrought iron rail to land on the ground, five floors below.

Seeing someone else cumming always gets me off, and seeing him unload so much—and so far—sent me over the edge. For the first time in my life, I tried cumming as he had, without stroking myself. To my surprise, it worked. It felt great, watching a stream of jizz shoot five or six times, then ooze down the shaft of my dick.

Across the courtyard, my neighbor was shaking the last few drops of his load onto the balcony floor. He smiled a toothy grin, waved good-bye and walked back into his hotel room, then immediately closed the curtains.

Two orgasms in one day was more than I'd had in quite a while. I mean, we all whacked off over in the deserts of Afghanistan—you *had* to, just to keep sane. Especially for me, being gay and surrounded by so many hot, hunky marines. I can still conjure up images of my favorite jack-off-fantasy guys, the ones I'd watch in the showers and later imagine having my way with, sucking on those awesome cocks or fucking their amazing asses.

The next day, I went to the local army and navy surplus store and picked up a pair of binoculars. The next time my exhibitionist friend put on a show for me, I decided, I was going to get a good, up-close look at him.

During the day, I spent time at the pool in a new swimsuit that I thought showed off my attributes well. By late afternoon, I'd gotten enough sun that I was bronzed all over—except for the part covered by the suit, which I planned to take care of the following day on a visit to the nude beach a little further up the coast.

That night, I checked outside my window several times to see if my sexy neighbor was putting on an encore performance. I was still in my swimsuit, with a polo shirt I'd thrown on before going down to the hotel's restaurant for dinner. I'd had a couple of drinks after my meal, so I was feeling fine and ready for action. But at 19:00, 19:30 and 20:00, he wasn't there. Half an hour later, I noticed him sitting on his balcony, talking on his cell phone. He was completely turned out in his dress blues, clearly a fellow marine. Dressed like that, he must have gone to some big event at Camp Pendleton, up the coast in Oceanside. I pulled out my binoculars to get a better look.

He was stunningly attractive. I'd already seen the blond hair and well-developed body, but now I could make out his steel-blue eyes, his Roman nose, and his very sexy dimples. His hair was loosely curled, making him look almost like a statue of Adonis.

Only Adonis was *naked* in that statue, and that's how I wanted to see him again.

A man in a well-fitting uniform is incredibly sexy to me, and this guy's fit him like a second skin. From head to toe, he was amazing. And when he smiled, his teeth were brilliantly white, set off so handsomely against his surfer-like tanned skin.

I was as easy to spot as a Pashtun in Afghanistan, standing there with my binoculars trained on him. He ended his phone call, smiled at me, and went back inside, closing the sheer curtains in his room. With all the lights, I could see him in silhouette.

He began undressing. Party time was about to start again!

A few minutes later, the curtains parted and he emerged wearing nothing but a jockstrap. Holy shit! He looked incredibly hot. That amazing body of his, along with his porn-star cock stuffed in that little jock, made me hard immediately.

I stood inside my room, behind the sliding glass doors, watching him through my binoculars as he picked up a beer from the small table on the balcony and took a swig. He motioned for me to open the door and come outside. I shook my head. I wasn't ready for that. But I did take off my shirt for him, which he responded to with a thumbs up gesture and a squeeze of his package.

I held up one finger, signaling for him to wait, and then slowly wriggled out of my swimsuit. Now naked before him, I leaned against the window, pressing my hardening cock against the glass, and moved and down to give him a good look at my equipment. He smiled that perfect Adonis smile and again held onto his meat through his jock. I noticed the fat tip of his dick sticking up from the waistband. My little show was having its intended effect.

Stepping back, I picked up the binoculars and trained them on him, taking note of his beautiful eyes, his perfect teeth, his bulging pecs, and that fantastic trail of blond hair that led from his navel down into that well-stuffed jock. His cock was snaking up toward his stomach; it was now at least three inches above the waistband of his jock, making that swollen uncut head clearly visible.

He leaned casually against the balcony railing, as if being seen in public with one's cock peeking out of a jockstrap was the most natural thing in the world. I took in the whole amazing picture and felt a sensation almost like an electric shock strike at the base of my dick. If I wasn't careful, I might just cum without touching myself again.

He was fully hard now and, ever so slowly, he slipped the jockstrap down his legs, exposing at least nine inches of throbbing meat that stuck up at a forty-five-degree angle. Through the binoculars, I could see the thick veins pulsing along that beautiful shaft.

While I'm no porn star in the dick department, I've never heard any complaints. I'm just a little longer than average, with average thickness—nowhere near as big as my exhibitionist friend across the way. But he seemed to enjoy watching me slowly jack my dick, and soon he was doing the same. As I watched him, I gripped my cock tightly, enjoying the sensation of hot blood pulsing through the veins on the top of my shaft.

He pinched his erect nipples with his left hand as he let his right hand glide up and down his thick tool. With me watching through my binoculars and him continuing to smile that incredible smile, we both sped up the rhythm of our strokes, until our hands were just a blur running the length of our dicks. Once again, I felt like I could cum at any time. But I wanted to wait until my neighbor was ready, so I loosened my grip a bit and kept stroking in tandem with him.

Soon, he arched his back and I knew his eruption would soon follow, so I picked up speed and squeezed my cock firmly, giving myself four or five more strokes that took me to the edge. Still standing behind the sliding door, I shot my load onto the glass. Little streams of my seed ran down the surface. That was enough to get him off, and he came again, as hard and as far as he'd done the night before—launching a volley of cum over the side of the balcony. I smiled as I imagined what passing hotel guests would think if his load splashed on the walkway in front of them.

I continued to watch as he again shook the last few drops of his load onto the balcony floor, then looked across at me and gave me another wide grin. He picked up his beer, offered that salute as he raised the bottle above his head, then turned and walked back into his room.

I went to the bathroom to get a washcloth to clean up the mess I'd made on the balcony's door, and when I looked across the courtyard again, his curtains were closed.

Three orgasms in two days was a good start for me, and I still had several days left to visit the nude beach, the local leather bar, and even a bathhouse in the city. Plus there was always a chance I could get Ted to come back to my room again in his sexy uniform. So, I was certain this would be a trip I'd remember long after I'd bid San Diego, and my exhibitionist friend, a fond good-bye. I was ready for anything.

Semper fi!

KAMIKAZE JOURNO SEEKS TROOP LEADER

Roger Willoughby

"Have you ever attended a boy scout orgy? Well, I have, and it's fucking in *tents*."

OK, so I'm a better journalist than a joke teller. Maybe because I'm a happy joke teller and an angry journalist. But it's the anger that gets results. See, I've had it up to here with this bullshit about scouts discriminating against gay kids. It's not right. Not that it's a personal issue for me or anything. You don't have to be gay to care about injustice. As a journalist, my sexual preference is irrelevant. Just like Anderson Cooper's used to be. So, I won't tell you which side of the fence I play on, except to say that I don't like labels of any kind. But this is an issue that should be important to everyone. Because when one of us suffers from discrimination, we all suffer. So, I've decided that what's needed is an exposé. I know for a *fact* there are plenty of gay scout leaders. And if I can catch one of them red-handed, say, in the act of blowing someone (or better!), I think I can blow the lid off of this whole thing in a big way.

I'm a man on a mission. Unfortunately, due to the sensitivity of said mission, I myself have to act as bait. I can't very well hire a professional to seduce someone. How the hell am I getting to get a publisher to reimburse me for that? I remember hearing about a colleague who wrote a piece on drug trafficking and tried to file an expense report for fifteen grand's worth of coke. Stupid. They weaseled out of paying him on a technicality: He didn't submit an original receipt. Now, I could probably hire a rent boy to go in there and fuck a scout leader in the ass, but last I heard, rent boys prefer cash up front to invoicing.

Which means I'm going it alone on this one. You can always tell a good journalist by what he's willing to do to get a story. And I'll do whatever it takes. Even if it's not my cup of tea.

Getting your hands dirty is just one aspect of a good journo's day at the office. Another is research. Thankfully this is also an area in which I excel. I know, for example, that there's a scout camping trip this weekend up at the lake's east end. I can even tell you the focus of this particular outing: fire building skills. I also know from my extensive nosing around (and not from personal experience, as I was never a scout myself) that at night, after the fires have gone out, there's always one scout leader whose job it is to stay up and keep watch over the campsite. This is when I'll make my move. That way, if things get sticky (and from what I hear, they will), it won't happen in front of the kiddies because they'll be safely tucked in their tents dreaming about their fire badges.

It's a perfect plan: On Saturday night I'll make my way up to the lake's east end, wait until everyone has gone to sleep, and then jump headfirst into the field, as we journalists like to say. I'll seduce whatever scout leader is stuck on the night watch and let him do whatever he wants to me. (All for the sake of a good story, of course.) Then I'll write the piece and wait for it go global!

Saturday night. Twelve thirty a.m. I'm armed with the necessary journalist's supplies: video camera, still camera, notepad, condoms, and lube. And a butt plug, just in case. (You never know what will happen. "Be prepared," as the scouts say.) Making my may to the lake's east end, I walk carefully through the brush, trying not to wake any of the sleeping scouts.

The walk is longer than I'd expected, but a journalist doesn't complain. He just treks on. Even if it means a ten-minute hike from the edge of civilization.

Up ahead I see a light: Bingo! Moving in closer and perching myself behind a large tree, I discover the illumination's source: a scout-issued lantern.

It's then that I see him. He's sitting on a tree stump, and even from a distance, I can see that he's the perfect representation of the American scout leader. And what a handsome one he is, too. He looks a lot like Prince Harry: red hair, pale skin, and tall and lean. On top of his head is an olive green scout hat, perfectly in place. His tan shirt is covered in badges that I recognize from my research (campsite service, paddle sports, hill walker, arts enthusiast, etc.) and has red-looped epaulets on the shoulders. His green neckerchief sits neatly in a V below his neck in the very center of his shirt, covering the buttons. Below the waist he sports olive green shorts that match the hat.

He looks to be around twenty-five years old and boasts a clean face and hands, just as it says to in the scout handbook. The only thing not-by-the-book is the cock in his hand. I can see very clearly from my post that while he's left the top button on his shorts fastened, he's unzipped the zipper and pulled out his bone, which he's stroking. This does *not* seem very scout-like. If his tribemaster ever happened upon this, his career would be over for sure. (Just as it will be when I'm done exposing him, which I see now will be easier than I thought!)

To get his attention, I make a rustling noise in the trees.

"Who goes there?" he asks, letting go of his prick, which I can see now, as it swings back and forth, is quite large.

"It's Franky," I say. (I picked Franky as my undercover name because it sounds nonthreatening. If I'd said my name was Angelo or LeRoy or something ethnic, I might have aroused suspicion.) "I'm just passing through the woods but I've lost my way. Can you help me?"

I watch as he quickly stuffs his prick back into his shorts. It takes some effort to get the thing back in there. "Um, sure …" he says, sounding flustered.

I walk out from behind the tree, making myself visible to him. "What are you doing out here all by yourself?" I ask.

"I'm not alone," he says quickly as he jumps from the tree stump. "I'm a scout master, braving the woods to keep watch over a bunch of scouts who are sleeping in nearby tents, sir!" Oddly, he salutes me. (Does he think I'm a marine?)

I look at his crotch, which is sporting an impressive tent of its own. "It doesn't look like anything's asleep on you," I say, stepping up to him. I can feel his breath on my face as my hand reaches out and grips his bulge. My touch practically makes him buckle at the knees.

A look of shock registers on his face. "What are you doing?" he asks without pulling away.

"I'm feeling your cock," I say. "No wait—" I add immediately, dropping to my knees and pulling his zipper down. I pull his hard bone out of his tighty-whities. It *is* big, surrounded by a neatly trimmed spattering of ginger pubic hair, and it throbs in my hand. "—I'm *sucking* your cock."

I take the thing in my mouth, at first just the head, which I gently wrap my lips around and then circle with my tongue. He moans as I slowly envelop more and more of his long shaft. I try and swallow

48

the thing (there's nothing I won't do for a good story), but there's just too much of it.

Undeterred, I continue to feast on the thing, making slurping noises as I go. After slowly sliding his shorts and underwear down, I reach my hands around him so I can cup his ass. It feels surprisingly muscular. Gripping his cheeks, I pull his whole body slightly forward, pushing his prick deeper into my mouth, then pull him back, taking it a few inches out. I do this a few times until he takes the lead and begins rhythmically fucking my mouth. It's then that I know I've got him right where I want him.

I stop abruptly, letting go of his ass and letting his dick fall from my mouth. "Mmmmm," he moans, "don't stop."

Grabbing his shaft, I slowly guide the head back into my mouth. This time I vow to take the whole thing, so inch by inch I ease it past my lips. It seems easier this time. When my lips reach my hand I'm pretty proud of myself. I bob back and forth a few strokes, then pull my hand away as I continue to swallow. When I feel the swollen head of his mini-scout caress my uvula, I know I'm getting close to earning a deep throat badge.

But then he stops me. "You're gonna make me cum," he says in a whisper. He takes a step back, letting his prick fall from my mouth and then pulls me to my feet. I immediately feel something on my nipples. Glancing down, I see that the scout leader is pinching them. This is my weakness, but he couldn't possibly have known that. His long fingers begin unbuttoning my shirt, which he then slides over my shoulders and pushes off me. The next thing I know, he's frantically sucking on my left nipple, gently biting it. It feels incredible as it hardens in his mouth. This could make *me* cum, but I haven't yet completed my mission so I gently push him away.

Undeterred, he reaches his hand down and grips the crotch of my camouflage pants. My meat is hard. "What have we here?" he asks, as if he didn't know. "I might have to take a closer look …"

When he unbuttons and unzips me, my camos drop to the forest floor. I'm not wearing underwear (as a writer, I like alliteration, so "camouflage" and "commando" seemed like a clever combo), so he has easy access to my manhood, which is standing up proud.

He does indeed go for a closer look. As he takes me in his mouth, his hand reaches down and gently cups my balls. Tugging downward on them, he begins licking my shaft, up and down like a lollipop, then suddenly he's gulping the whole thing. Feeling a tickling in my groin area, I look down and see the scout leader's face buried in my pubic hair. My entire prick is in his mouth! Clearly he's had a lot of practice at this. I start to hump his mouth, using my hips to thrust as hard as I can. But he pulls off.

"Don't," he says, again in a whisper. "I don't want you to cum yet either. Do you have a rubber?"

Of course I do. A reporter is always prepared. Just like a scout. I reach into my bag and pull out a string of five. (I wasn't sure how many this mission would require.) He laughs as he tears one off.

"Do you want to be inside me?" he asks. I nod, not sure how eager I should play this. He tears open the foil packet and rolls it on me. "We're gonna need lube."

I have that in my bag as well. And again he laughs as I pull it out. (I didn't have time to buy a travel-size, so I'd grabbed the jumbo bottle with the pump that lives on my bedside table.) I squirt some into his hand and drop the bottle back into the bag. He rubs the lube onto my hard dick while stroking it. It feels so good.

"How do you want me?" he asks.

"Bent over that," I say, referencing the tree stump he'd earlier been wanking himself on. He grabs his neckerchief and begins to lift it over his head, but I hold out my hand in protest. "Leave the rest of the uniform on," I say.

He shrugs. "OK."

The tree stump is the perfect height for him to bend over. Admiring his muscular ass, I caress his cheeks with my hand, then reach down between his legs to spread them apart. Using my other hand, I grab my monster meat and slide it into his hole.

"Ooooh, that's good," he pants, cocking his head up at an odd angle in order to look at me.

I could cum right now; the feeling of being inside this studly scout leader (and knowing what a good story this will end up being!) is pushing me to the edge. But I slowly ease my way in as far as I can go, then hold it there for a few seconds before pulling out, which I do all the way.

"Put it back in me!" he shouts, oblivious to the sleeping scouts.

I look down at his twitching hole. It's stretched open and waiting for my prick, so I position the head at the edge of his pussy lips and ram it back in hard.

"*Yes!* That's fuckin' great!" he screams. "*Fuck my hole!*"

At this point I'm a little uncomfortable. I'd hate for his volume to summon a bear, or worse yet, a member of law enforcement. Having my limbs ripped from my body by a wild beast or being arrested for indecent exposure would *not* be a good ending to my exposé. "Dude, take a down a notch," I say.

"OK, sorry," he says breathlessly. I ram his ass again, even harder this time. "*Fuuuuuuuuuuuuuuuuuck!*" he whispers. That's better.

I grab hold of the back of his scout shirt and pull it like the reins on a horse as I continue to make his hole happy. Before I realize it, I'm cumming, shooting my wad deep into his guts. Now I'm the one going "*Fuuuuuuuuuuuuuuuuuuck!*"

For a second, I forget what I'm there for, lost as I am in the heat of the moment. Because after I cum, the next thing I see is the scout leader, on his feet, shooting thick gobs of man juice all over my chest. The sensation is warm and it feels good. Spent, he collapses into me, his semen adhesing the two of us together.

When he finally pulls his adorable self away from me, he says, "I thought you were going to take pictures. What happened?"

I grimace. "I totally forgot. Got caught up in the moment. Ditto for the butt plug."

"Oh, that sucks. I love butt plugs."

"What happened to Larry?" I ask.

"Couldn't make it. He injured his foot as a hockey player. He didn't realize it required ice skating." He makes an *oh-my-God-how-stupid-is-he?* face as he offers his hand for a shake. "I'm Peter."

"Evan," I say as my hand meets his. "Nice to meet you. How long have you been with GayUniformFantasy.com?"

"A few months. But this was my first time on this side. I was a little nervous."

"Really? I totally couldn't tell."

His face melts. "You're so sweet! Hey, do you want to 'friend' me? Maybe you could role-play for me next time ..."

"Sure. What are you thinking?"

"You promise you won't laugh?"

I shake my head. "Of course not. What could be cheesier than a scout leader fantasy?"

"I've always wanted to be abducted by an alien."

I smile and once again put my hand on his muscular ass cheek. "I could totally get into that ..."

Wait, I've got one more: "Why did the scout leader get arrested while camping? Because he was loitering within tent ..."

BURN

Gregory L. Norris

The first orgasm, burning white-hot, instantly overwhelmed Corin, forcing his body to straighten out, transforming him from a bent shadow hiding among the boulders and trees to an actual body, visible, out in the open. Fresh sweat broke across his flesh. The temperature on that merciless muggy day, now waning to night, skyrocketed. Corin forgot to breathe. His tongue shriveled. His throat ached for water. All of the liquid inside him had leached through his pores or squirted out of his cock to ooze down the inside of his leg. He was on fire.

Corin's misery had started the moment he set forth down Dean Avenue. By Palomino, his blue jeans had rubbed his tick-tocking cock to within a few strokes of cumming. His balls had felt itchy and loose before leaving the apartment. His nerves had been on edge in anticipation since he received the knowledge, and when he long last shot his load into the front of his too-tight jeans—because he had bravely traveled to this place, he was *here*—every cell in his body climaxed in appreciation.

Then the wave finished its crash over him, and he was just one more horny male soaked in sweat with his dick hanging out among the rangy pines near the exit 2 rest area sandwiched between the highway and the woods off Palomino Drive. More to the point, he was now fair game, an easy target.

Corin struggled to catch his breath and choked down the ball of heat gathered at the back of his mouth. He didn't see any other men but had heard things—snapping branches, a grunt, car doors opening and closing quietly, secretively down in the patch of pitted asphalt visible through breaks in the branches. The woods had a mossy end-of-summer odor, stale in a way that reminded him of the locker room at his high school—a smell Corin still equated with sex a year and two months after graduation.

What if Larry had lied about the woods off Palomino Drive? The fucker, Corin knew too well, delighted in making his life miserable. Corin had been at the bottom of the pecking order in high school, and not much had changed since. He was still being picked on and teased by the local bully, only now that bully paid him three bucks, thirty-five cents an hour for the privilege and wore a nametag with the word MANAGER on it.

Just go home before you get into trouble, the sane voice in his thoughts urged.

Corin shuffled a few steps forward. Another, less sane representative from his imagination piped up, reminding him that he hadn't come this far just to ejaculate a mess into his underwear. *You could have done that in your bed, under your sheet, man.* Or in a sock, or down the shower drain, or out behind the sagging gray metal shed behind the apartment complex where they stored the lawn equipment.

What Corin had traveled to accomplish involved activities requiring two participants.

"Hey," a gruff man's voice said from Corin's right in that part of the woods suddenly gone gray.

54

Corin spun around. The jarring motion briefly sent the world into a cyclone of charcoal tones, launched electricity down his legs, up his torso, the current supplied by his cock, which had stiffened again fully. The world stabilized enough for Corin to see that the man was, indeed, a man. Tall, dressed in a T-shirt and cut-off shorts, sneakers, and white tube socks. The man wore his hair in a buzz cut, looked tough, masculine, and had a mustache.

It's him, one of the voices, sane or insane, clarioned in his thoughts. It didn't matter whether they were right or if the man was really fire-fighter Tom Mankins; in the twilight, the man became Tom.

"Hi," Corin said around a mouthful of hot coals.

The man shifted in place, snaked a big hand, hairy on the back, down to grope his crotch. "You up for it?"

A curious mix of apprehension and excitement slithered over Corin's skin. "Sure," he stammered.

Several tense seconds later, the fireman huffed, "What are you waiting for? Get over here and suck my dick."

"Yeah, right," Corin heard himself say, adding a nervous chuckle. But the voice didn't sound like his own any more than his body felt under his control. Corin shuffled forward, taking awkward, leaden steps. Sweat poured down his forehead and stung at his eyes. After crossing the few yards—what felt more like a gulf of miles—Corin dropped to his knees. He gazed up, high on a heady cocktail of cologne and crotch.

"That's a good boy," the man growled.

"I'm nineteen. I'm not a boy."

"Less yapping and more sucking. I don't got a lot of time."

Sane absently wondered if the man was a trucker, driver of one of the big rigs parked at the rest stop. Insane, the voice in Corin's head that worried he was broken, defective, an abomination, told him *no,* this man was Tom Terrific, Tom Mankins, the friendly neighborhood fireman, mustache and all.

Hands shaking, Corin unhooked the man's belt, unbuttoned him, unzipped. He wasn't wearing underwear. *Free-balling it,* as Corin had once heard a coworker say at the Burger Shack. It was hot out, real dog day weather, Sane reasoned. It didn't strike him at first that the man wasn't wearing his tight-whites because he was, in truth, old hat at this, a frequent visitor to the regional suck-and-squirt, not until the long walk back to the apartment.

Right then, however, eyes wide and unblinking, Corin focused on the god's cock. Gorged on blood, it log-rolled out of his shorts to hang at an angle, its shaft bent in the middle, its head a classic helmet whose piss-hole had already begun to leak. Two enormous balls spilled out beneath it, ripe with that funky locker room odor Corin loved. Lush curls wreathed everything.

Corin gripped the man's cock by its root and leaned closer. His next orgasm snuck up on him as secretively as the first, right as he stole his initial taste of the fireman's boner. The ripe male taste, the spongy texture … how often he'd rubbed his erection in the dark, or outside behind the shed, hidden from prying eyes, dreaming of this moment. Dreaming of that *uniform.* And here it was, long last—with the man of his dreams.

"I love you, Tom," Corin moaned around the man's dick while also tugging at his balls. The new night filled with exploding stars that only he could see and Corin came without touching himself.

"Watch your teeth, boy," the man admonished. He no longer sounded like Tom Mankins, any more than he sounded pleased at the job Corin was doing. And he wasn't in his fireman's uniform.

A rush of guilt and disgust flooded Corin's insides. The truth glared at him. He was on his knees in the woods, sucking on a stranger's cock. Said stranger's smell made him gag. And the taste…would he ever be able to wash it off his tongue? The most damning evidence was the knowledge of who the man was *not.*

For a brief and startling instant, Corin was at work, standing outside the Burger Shack, with seven of his coworkers and that arrogant toad, Larry Hinsdale. Corin's heart raced. Not because of the fire alarm, wailing from inside the restaurant—the term *restaurant* being generous, as the appropriately named Burger Shack, the B. S. was, indeed, a shack. Not owing to the deep bleats pulsing from the fire truck, the town's behemoth red pumper. Or the flurry of uniformed bodies tracking back and forth between the smoke-filled building, the ambulance, or police cruiser that had responded. Not even Larry's cries of vengeance against the entire crew, which he threatened to can, regardless of who started the grease fire. After he lit *them* on fire, of course, and pissed out the ashes.

No, what caused Corin's heart to gallop was the image of the tall, handsome hero who jumped out of the pumper wearing big rubber boots and a black and yellow coat over a tight-fitting black T-shirt. A man with a sculpted athlete's haircut and a trim black mustache.

Corin tracked the man's course, around the pumper and into the restaurant. He imagined what it would be like to still be inside, crying out for help, and to be rescued by this man, this god, this—

This cock painting his tongue in pre-cum was not Tom Mankin's.

Corin spit it out, licked his lips, shuddered. "I have to go," he said and started to rise, only to get slammed back down.

"You're not done yet, cocksucker," the brute growled. "Lick my nuts."

"No," Corin protested.

The man seized a handful of sweaty hair. "You ain't allowed to stop until you finish getting me off, fuck face."

Ripe, sweaty balls smashed against his nostrils and lips.

"Suck them!"

Corin did, afraid that a clout—or worse—would follow if he disobeyed. The man's nuts were too big to gobble at the same time so he hard-sucked the left first, then the right. They were oily with stale sweat, stunk of raw masculinity. Corin attempted to convince himself they were Tom's balls. Big, handsome Tom, his man in uniform. His hero. It worked, at least for a time, and he was back in the parking lot outside the Burger Shack. Larry continued his tirade.

"Fire you all, sue your asses, too—only I doubt I'd get much from a bunch of titty-babies who still live at home with their mommies." Larry delivered that last bit directly at Corin. "Some of you losers who don't even live in real houses!"

Corin hated Larry, had hated him dating back to the previous autumn of '82, when he was hired on the spot at minimum wage plus one meal per full shift.

"Hey, leave that kid alone," a man's deep voice interjected.

Larry's outburst ended, and Corin turned toward the source of the voice. It was the fireman with the mustache, standing with his ax in hand, his jacket opened just enough to reveal a hint of sweat blossoming out of armpits.

"This isn't *his* fault," the fireman said, his voice powerful enough to shut lousy Larry Hinsdale's mouth.

The fireman's blue-gray gaze shifted toward Corin. The man continued on his way to the pumper, but not before offering the barest smile. Mouth hanging open, Corin could only stare, drinking in the perfect square of the fireman's butt in his uniform pants, the size of his feet, the sweat glistening on his neatly-shorn neck.

My hero, thought Corin.

"You little cock-smooch," Larry grumbled.

But Corin didn't care. He was in love. For the first time, really, truly in love.

"Suck it."

The vision shorted out, this time completely, as the length invading his mouth slid deeper, tapping the back of his throat. Corin gagged. Tears invaded his eyes. He coughed. The man with the mustache seemed to enjoy this development more than anything else. The cock between his lips swelled up even thicker, taking on a consistency like stone. A succession of ruthless fuck-thrusts forward left Corin choking, unable to breathe. Bile shuddered up his throat, but it was driven back down in a flood of salty, sour liquid. The man with the mustache whispered a moan as he came. Corin swallowed the mouthful of sperm and fantasized that it belonged to Tom.

The man pulled out, sighed in disgust. Hauling up his shorts, he hawked a wad of spit and launched it at Corin. The spit struck his cheek. Fear surged back in a paralyzing dose. Corin remained where he was and didn't so much as raise a hand to ward off the mosquitoes buzzing around his head or wipe at the brand of spittle, not until he heard the man's footsteps crunching across the forest floor, headed in the direction of the parking lot. Only then did he move.

Corin raced down the trail and back onto Palomino Drive, and didn't stop running until he'd reached the neighborhood containing the drab red brick apartment buildings. Soaked in sweat and convinced he was going to catch fire and spontaneously combust, Corin hot-footed into the front entrance of Building R, up the stairs, and down the long, dark hallway. Steeling himself, he unlocked the door to 2-09.

The apartment was unbearably hot and smelled of her sweat. She was asleep on the sofa, in front of the TV. Corin crept past her and to his bedroom. Though little else that night had gone smoothly, this one thing did, and he was grateful. He made it into his room and closed the door, thought about turning on the air conditioner but decided not to—the noise would wake her and then he'd catch hell for running up the electricity bill.

Instead, he opened the windows, sweated, and stunk, the musky odor on his body both his own and that of the stranger in the woods.

Before shutting off the light and stripping down, Corin opened the little calendar book he kept in the bedside table's drawer and flipped back two months to June the 27th, 1983, a date circled with a heart in bold red ink.

The day Tom Mankins saved them all at the Burger Shack and stole Corin's heart.

Corin needed rescuing.

From the Burger Shack, where he had become the manager's favorite punching bag; where, two nights earlier while swabbing out the men's restroom during the final hour of the closing shift Larry had said, "What's taking you so long? You in there giving blow jobs? Don't you know most of the fags in this town go down to the woods near the rest stop for that?"

From her, now out in the kitchen slamming cabinets and plates, her usual morning tirade. And cooking bacon again, if the sickening aroma in the air was any indication. The sun streaming into his room had already baked the place into an oven. Sweat and bacon. Worse, Corin still had that funky taste in his mouth. His stomach burbled. Corin exhaled, buried his face in his pillow, breathed through his nose. Nothing helped.

Most of all, Corin needed rescuing from himself.

He knew he liked men, not girls, even before puberty. But right after his body suffered the change signaling adulthood, at the back of his mind nagged a belief that there was something fundamentally wrong with him. A little crazy? Perhaps. Obsessive? Sure. Completely cuckoo-bird in the gray matter? There were mornings like the one after he'd sucked a complete stranger's cock and balls in the woods near the highway when he believed it.

Bacon. Corin gagged, willed his rising gorge to settle, and held his breath. Owing to the greasy meals his mother cooked, his job at the

Burger Shack, and the fact he'd caught Larry Hinsdale spitting onto an unruly customer's double-stack with extra tomatoes, Corin had renounced eating meat. He was now a vegetarian, four months and less than a week along.

Of course, he'd devoured meat last night, one of the voices in his head teased. He'd swallowed animal product—the dude's load—so what did that make him now?

"A cocksucker," Corin whispered into the pillow, aware of the wicked little smile creeping onto his lips.

True, the man with the mustache wasn't Tom Mankins. But, for an instant, Corin had believed he was.

"Tom," he sighed. Then he was hard again and itchy all over, stroking his cock and fantasizing.

The gods had seen fit to put him in the drive-thru window a few weeks earlier, on a Saturday night. Corin almost never manned the window; by a fluke, that particular night, the lines of fate crossed and, at five o'clock, a black truck drove up to the speaker.

"Welcome to the Burger Shack. What can I get you?"

Never before had a double-stack, fries, and cola, no ice, sounded so poetic after Corin connected the deep, manly baritone over the speaker with the rugged firefighter who pulled up to the window. A cold knife flayed him down the middle, gullet to gonads, while fresh sweat broke across his forehead.

"Hi," Corin stammered.

Sitting behind the wheel of the pickup dressed in his fireman's uniform and looking more like a force of nature than anyone mortal was the handsome hero who'd come to Corin's rescue back on that miserable June night.

"Hey, buddy, how's it hanging?"

Suddenly, there were multiple Corins in the drive-thru window: the insane version, whose eyes wandered down the sculpt of the man's chest, lower, to the fullness of his crotch, the bulge of a real man's cock and meaty balls clearly displayed in his uniform pants; the sane one, who rang in the man's order, tendered change, and offered a reserved smile; and the Corin who was a bit of both, sane and insane, and completely, totally in love with this magnificent defender of the downtrodden.

"You saved us, back in June. June the 27th. I remember it well."

The fireman shrugged. "I just helped put out your grease fire, that's all."

"Naw, it was more than that. You were great. Thanks."

"You're welcome."

"Corin," he heard himself answer. "Corin Smith."

The man in the fireman's uniform—the *god*—extended his hand. "Tom Mankins, at your service, buddy."

Corin hesitated. For a moment, all he could do was focus on that hand. The hand of a true god, so strong, with its rough skin, the pattern of dark hair sprouted across its back; those fingers, which scratched the god's hairy balls and wiped his ass and jerked his cock and picked the sock fuzz from between his sweaty toes …

Corin reached for it and the effect, he imagined, was like that famous painting by Michelangelo in the Sistine Chapel, *God Creates Adam*. Their flesh connected. Tom squeezed down and Corin felt born again.

He also shot his wad into his pants, right then and there in the drive-thru window.

"Where were you last night?"

"Work."

"I called work. You weren't in."

Corin drank his glass of water; his stomach couldn't handle orange juice—or her interrogation. "Whoever you talked to lied."

She snorted a piggy laugh, shifted on the sofa. "Then we'll see when you get paid. Don't think I won't know."

The stench of bacon grease infused the apartment. Corin swept a look around the dirty builder-beige walls, across the cheap glass-top kitchen table, the stack of unopened bills, and made it into the living room. His eyes drifted over the dirty brown sectional, where she sat stuffing her face and watching the TV, only to deflect away, to the wall, where a lone photo was hung, that of a handsome man dressed in a suit and tie; a man with a neat, full mustache.

Corin broke focus with the photograph and hurried away before the despair of it all completely smothered him to death.

Another merciless scorcher baked the morning. By afternoon, Corin couldn't breathe and was convinced he'd catch fire and burn up. He'd already showered twice and jerked off to visions of Tom Mankins an equal number of times. He had to get away from the apartment.

Corin headed toward the front door.

"Where are you going?"

"For a walk."

"Don't you have to work?"

"Not today. Schedule's on the fridge, remember?"

"Call up Mister Hinsdale and tell him you want overtime. We've got bills to pay. Phone, cable, groceries—*the rent*. And tell him you want a raise!"

Corin yes'ed her and kept walking. He exited one miserable realm and entered another outside the building. The blanket of humidity engulfed him, making his steps heavier despite their quickness. Corin hurried down Dean Avenue, headed who-knew-where under the power of his own footfalls when most guys his age drove cars.

What he wouldn't give to drive around town in the passenger seat of that big black pickup truck beside the man in the fireman's uniform. Then nobody would nark on him—they wouldn't dare, because they'd know he was Tom Terrific's special buddy.

The plan came to him several days later, while Corin lay sprawled across his bed in his underwear, listening to Duran Duran on the radio. He'd been daydreaming the time away through numerous romantic scenarios, oblivious to the hour: Tom Mankins rescuing him, carrying him out of a burning building straight to the safety of his bed, where the fireman gazed deeply into his eyes and, unable to resist, fucked him in a variety of holes and positions. The smell of smoke carried around his hero in Corin's fantasies, the raw, primal stink of creation and destruction.

Corin sucked on Tom's bare toes, licked his hairy balls, feasted upon Tom's asshole, now knowing how those places on a man's body would taste. They were universal, pretty much the same on all of the men he'd serviced who weren't Tom. But on Tom, their ripeness, their musk, was gloriously pure to him because he was Tom, Terrific Tom, Corin's champion. For Tom, who pulled him to safety when his car ran off a road, slammed into a tree; who caught Corin when he jumped off the balcony and into his powerful arms; who punched Larry Hinsdale in the face, swept Corin into his protective embrace, and carried him out of the Burger Shack, pledging to take care of him forever on his fireman's paycheck, there was little he wouldn't give the man. Corin would lick and sniff every inch of Tom's body, no matter how sweaty or dirty, because that's what real men liked.

That's what *his* man liked.

The smoky smell of Tom filled his mind and his breaths, so vivid in the warm bedroom. All it would take to make the scenarios real was another small grease fire at the Burger Shack. Nothing too elaborate. The last one had only kept him out of work for a week for repairs. An alarm would clear the place out, preventing injuries.

The fire department would respond. Tom would again rescue him—from his rotten boss, that shitty job, this miserable life. They would leave together, and he'd never be forced to face the foul lump of flesh in the apartment's other rooms again.

He'd be with the man he loved forever.

"You idiot," the boss man shrieked.

Hinsdale shoved him away hard enough that Corin hit the fryolator. He reached on instinct to steady himself from falling, only to recoil at the rush of exquisitely painful heat up his hands as his fingers connected with the volcanic surface. Then he was on the floor among the grease and the french fries that had slipped between the counter and fryolator. The stench nearly overwhelmed him, but the agony of two seared fingertips kept him keenly aware of what happened next as Hinsdale banged out the small flames using a dishcloth.

"I saw you, you filthy little cock-biter," Hinsdale shouted, oblivious to customers and coworkers alike. "You set it deliberately with these!"

Hinsdale held up a book of matches, the ones Corin had taken from *her* clutter back at that hellish apartment.

"You tried to burn down the place—get the fuck out of here!"

"But—" Corin protested.

"Now! You're fired. And if you ever come in here again, I swear I'll fucking kill you!"

Fired. And failed.

His stomach in knots, two fingers on the hand he used to masturbate singing in pain, both with divots of flesh weeping sticky fluid where the blisters had popped, he walked up and down Dean Avenue, wondering where he should go. Corin attempted to apply at two different grocery stores, only at each place, the managers sized him up and down and said they weren't hiring, despite the signs on glass doors advertising to the contrary.

By the time he showed up at the fire station, Insane Corin was in control.

"Tom, yes, Tom."

"Tom who? Bishop or Mankins?"

"Tom Terrific," Corin said, his voice verging on sobs. "It's an emergency!"

"What kind of emergency?" asked the fireman standing near the big red pump truck, a chubby man with a bushy beard covered in flecks of dandruff. Even in his crazed state—maybe because of it—Corin sensed the note of condescension in the man's attitude, something Corin recognized all too clearly from school, from work, from life. From nineteen shitty years of life that felt more like ninety when you got right down to it.

"*Now,*" Corin shrieked. "Please ..."

The fireman snorted a swear beneath his breath and turned away from the colossal open garage door. The caustic sting of dry tears invaded the corners of Corin's eyes. He circled in place, waited for what felt more like hours than minutes.

But then Corin glanced up, and there he stood. Tom Terrific.

His Tom Terrific.

The room smelled like men, like sweaty ass and hairy balls and dirty gym socks. It was a lounge with a TV hooked up to a cable box, not rabbit ears, a bunch of newspapers turned to the sports pages, and a copy of a pawed-through beaver magazine.

"Burned my hand at work," Corin managed when Tom Terrific asked him what was wrong.

"You're that kid from the Burger Shack, right?"

Corin's mouth broke in a wide smile. "Yeah, you remember me?"

"Sure do," Tom Terrific said. "Let's have a look at that hand."

The sting as he cleaned Corin's fingers, applied salve, and wrapped them in special pads for burn wounds barely registered. The contours of the room no longer seemed solid. Corin caught himself staring at Tom, staring without blinking, completely bewitched by the fireman's magnificence. Corin breathed in the scent of sweat Tom exuded, clean and masculine. He studied Tom Terrific's mustache and lips, lips that curled downward when he smiled. Despite the pain of his touch, Tom's fingers sent icy-hot flickers rippling through Corin's blood.

"You gotta be more careful, buddy," Tom Terrific said. He gave Corin's knee a playful pat.

And then, with the line between fantasy not simply blurred beyond recognition but completely gone, Corin leaned up and crushed their lips together. The kiss lasted for a second, perhaps two, and filled Corin's head with a Fourth of July spectacle that only he could see. Flesh met flesh, the taste more delicious than Corin had thought possible, even in his most vivid fantasies. Their lips met, held—

Then Tom shoved him away, off the chair and onto the floor, right as Corin whispered the words, *"I love you, Tom."*

Crying. Spinning. Burning on the inside as well as the outside, he staggered back to the apartment, cursing himself for being so stupid. He'd kissed Tom—heaven! But hell had quickly followed, delivered by a shove from his mustached god's mighty hand. Tom. Tom had cast him out.

The tears left Corin feeling even drier on the inside, like kindling ready to ignite from the barest spark. Not even a week of rain or a gallon of icy water could put out that kind of conflagration once it started. It built steadier toward being; he felt the fire powering up, growing hotter with his steps. Tom could have saved him from those other men. He still could.

If only Hinsdale, the fucker, hadn't seen him tap the lit match to that pile of clotted fryolator fat splattered on the counter.

Still, it had been a very good plan.

It was still a very good plan.

She laid into him the moment he walked through the door.

"Hinsdale called, wants his uniform and nametag back before he'll give you your final paycheck. *Fired,* he said. You worthless piece of shit!"

She struck him across the face. Fresh pain crackled through his flesh, white-hot like summer thunder, the spark that lit the tinder. Now, there would only be flames.

Corin barely remembered shoving her, the doughy, loose feel of her filthy skin beneath his hands, or the sound of cracking furniture and bones as she tumbled over, hitting her skull on the TV stand. Even the peal of his scream emerged in a disconnected, distant way, someone else's voice, belonging to a worthless lump of flesh living in this squalor and being punished for the crimes others had committed.

But Corin had risen above that version of himself. He was the Phoenix, and he would ascend from the ashes. Tom would rescue him, see his beauty, heal him. Love him.

"Tom," Corin whispered.

Methodically, he glanced toward the phone, sitting atop the side table on a phone book. It had survived the destructive cyclone of spinning limbs and crashing furniture. Light the match. Touch it to the greasy stovetop. The curtains above the kitchen sink, too, which had absorbed plenty of oily residue over the years.

He lit another match and touched it to the roll of paper towels, the junk mail and bills piling up on the tacky department store table with the glass top, one of the four inserts missing, broken after she'd slammed her nasty coffee cup on it in a fit of anger over his meager weekly earnings.

Corin was so above her, above *this*. This shitty, miserable life. He deserved better. He deserved—

"Tom."

The smoky smell of his champion teased Corin's next sip of breath. Closing his eyes, he imagined Tom charging through the apartment door, desperate to rescue him, to be his big hero, to save the young man he loved. Corin would wrap an arm around Tom's neck, clinging to him for life. They would run through the flames together, forever in love, and they would make love nonstop. Hot, sweaty male love, tender as often as rough. Love and sex and endless, constant heat.

Tom's handsome face hovered before Corin's half-closed, dreamy gaze. He *had* come for him, as Corin knew his hero would. Tom loved him. That face, so handsome, so sexy ... his god's mustache, how it would feel tickling over his asshole as it feasted in readiness to fuck.

Then Corin realized he hadn't called 911 to ask for the fire department. He opened his eyes to see that the flames had jumped off the table, cut a line over the greasy floor, and were climbing the walls, devouring a cheap calendar, one she'd gotten free at the bank last Christmas. Christmas of 1982. A great Christmas, yeah—his gift had been locking himself in the bathroom while she drank and smoked and bemoaned her life. The calendar burned. So did the carpet.

Tom's face hovered out of focus beyond a filter of oily smoke. Corin focused. It wasn't Tom, savior of his universe, but the picture on the wall.

"Daddy?" Corin gasped.

He blinked, and the fantasy of Tom ended, leaving him surrounded by the stark reality of the flames.

Corin hurried toward the phone. Help—he needed to call for help! The grease on his shoes from his slip at the Burger Shack caught fire.

69

Flames raced up his pant leg. For a moment, he was the Phoenix, rising up from the ashes. But then the exquisite agony hit, and the hungry fire engulfed him.

OFFICER, INTERRUPTED

Brett Lockhard

After three years in Afghanistan, Adam Young returned to his hometown of Huntleigh, Missouri, a different man in many ways. Always considered a physical prize, Adam's lean soccer-trained body had grown in heroic proportions during his stint with the SEALs. Now a formidable 200 pounds of pure force, Adam was a vision of health, of raw animal virility. His body was not something that could have come out of a gym; there was no vanity in it, no sculptural perfection. This was a machine with purpose, an imposing vision of something beautiful and dangerous at once. He hadn't realized how much he had changed until he was dressing for his welcome-home dinner upon arriving. Standing at the closet, he reached for a plaid button-down shirt. Negotiating his outsized forearm through the sleeve was already a feat, but the rock hard bicep—now reaching eighteen inches around—proved impossible. The fabric split from shoulder to elbow along the seam as though scripted to symbolize his metamorphosis.

With the tattered shirt still unbuttoned, Adam turned to the mirror and examined himself almost in accusation. The crop of soft dark hair accentuated the burly mounds of his chest; it descended over the ridges of his natural abs toward the belt of his fatigues, suggesting something even more incredible below. Adam examined himself with a strange disillusionment about what this body now meant—how capable it was of violence and how dreadfully proud he was of its eerie accomplishments. It also, he was aware, had the capacity for great pleasure, although his talents in this regard had been rarely exercised over the past three years.

Adam threw his ruined shirt in the garbage and stood before the mirror deciding on his next steps. The dinner in his honor was only two hours away, and he had nothing that fit but his military garb. His crystal blue eyes were large and luminous, but when he looked at them, all he saw was a knowledge he wished he didn't have. Sadder than anything he had witnessed during the war was the realization that he wished he were back in Afghanistan—that it was all he knew now.

Adam sat on his bed, intimidated by everything ahead of him: all the mundane tasks, the blur of days and weeks that would pile on top of one another until his life had been lived. Shirtless, he looked in the mirror and, suddenly, as if succumbing, he accepted the small thrill that masturbation might bring.

He unzipped his pants and was surprised at how quickly his cock sprang to life. At twenty-six, he could still get off six or seven times a day if sufficiently bored. It was an opiate he was glad to deploy right now. The last time he'd had sex was over a year ago, but what he remembered of it was a balm he would regularly apply.

This memory began with only two soldiers left in the shower. Adam glanced sideways at Kevin, a friend he had seen soap up countless times. But never before had he noticed his thick eight-inch cock. A soldier's longing for human touch cannot be described in ordinary words, and "pent-up" does not begin to do justice to the charge in Adam's balls. For him, the yearning he suddenly felt was a nonnegotiable imperative—and one that was apparently mutual. Kevin reached a soapy hand under his balls, and his tool grew to fully hard. His arm tensed, producing ravines in his triceps as he slid a slick hand between the cheeks of his firm ass.

Adam felt a magnetic pull toward Kevin and the invitation he hoped he had not invented. His heart pounded as he made his way across the wet concrete floor. Standing inches apart, Adam stared directly into Kevin's eyes, saying nothing while making clear the pounding in store. There was no hesitation when he slipped three fingers into the tight hole; his authority was intoxicating, and Kevin, who showed such arrogant bravado in special missions, bent like a willow under Adam's spell.

Without a word, Adam kicked Kevin's legs apart and admired the sculptural ridges of his calves, the taut hamstrings that descended from his high, round ass. Kneeling behind him, Adam spread it apart to expose the anatomy of his delicious hole. He lurched forward and sent his tongue deep inside. Below, Adam's own cock—an imposing nine inches—was throbbing as the pre-cum poured.

With a massive forearm against the wood-plank walls, Kevin supported himself as best he could, though he feared his legs might buckle. Adam's hunger for this ass manifested in the most vigorous tonguing, opening Kevin's eager hole in preparation. There was a slow guttural moan—a dangerous but uncontrollable indulgence considering the rest of the troop just on the other side of the wall.

When Adam took Kevin from behind, his chest pressed against his back, they were bound by the slick surface of their skin. He wiped sweat from his forehead—when it mixed with the remnants of soap on his hand, he was able to work up just enough lather to qualify as lube. He stroked himself from head to base, then eagerly slid between the globes of Kevin's ass. He pushed slowly at first, feeling the maw envelop the tip of his dick, throbbing now.

Letting out a violently deep breath, Kevin made known that accepting the entirety of this gigantic member would not be easy. He reached his hand backward to hold Adam at the hip, communicating that he would need a few seconds before he could welcome the cock further inside. The slow expulsion of breath from his lungs made room for the feeling of need, letting Adam know that he was ready for more. Easing his way in, Adam was inebriated by the opening of the tight hole, a hungry thing that was suddenly so welcoming of every inch he could bury. As his hips finally pressed against Kevin's ass, Adam submitted to the intensity. The harsh desert reality around him blurred, and he was left only with the euphoric ascension toward orgasm.

The wave-like movement of his hips was gentle at first, his cock gliding smoothly, deeply, into the hole; still, he picked up speed with every thrust. Encouraging him, Kevin spread his legs even wider and leaned forward, sighing too loudly. He was a man satisfied beyond the point of caution. Adam reached for what the buzz cut had left of Kevin's blond hair. He pulled him by the neck and pushed his face against the fence.

"Look through the cracks, boy," Adam said. "Anyone else you feel like fucking? I'll invite them in right now. You know they've all had their eyes on you."

"No, sir."

"No, you haven't noticed …?"

"I've noticed, sir, but it's only you I want."

"Yeah?" Adam said, ripping harder into the hole.

"Sir, I want you to own me."

With that, Adam released a torturous pummeling. He let go of his head and planted both hands firmly on the small of his back, admiring the perfect V of the man's torso—a form that only good genes and youth could ever produce. Kevin's moans could not be contained, and

Adam knew that it was only minutes before someone walked through the door. It was not a fear of getting caught so much as a fear of being interrupted that goaded him toward the finish.

"You want my cum in you, boy?" Adam asked.

"More than anything," Kevin said, his words hampered by the incredible intensity of this fuck. "Shoot it deep in me," he said.

Obedient soldier that he was, Adam did as he was told and let loose an incredible load. Kevin was already close, but the flood of hot cum coating his ass made him breathless with urgent desire. Sensing the undeniable need, still fully hard inside him, Adam began yanking expertly. It only took a few strokes.

Back in his bedroom, as the memory of Kevin's load erupted in Adam's mind, he caught another glimpse of himself in his mirror. He wondered briefly how many times he had jerked off in front of it, how full this room was with episodes of filth. He wondered how other men saw his cock—a daily fact for him but an impressive delight for everyone who discovered it.

Adam thought about how it swelled in his hand before he spewed. His neck tensed in thick cords as he craned to watch himself unload. In the reflection he saw four gigantic wads reach high and land in various coordinates on his ripped abs. He would never know how other people saw him—an instrument of formidable power and rough beauty. Right now he only recognized the impossible relief of reliving a fuck that would exist forever in his memory—something he would revisit time and time again. It was a triumph he accepted might never be rivaled.

Motivated to make the mile-long trip to the mall to get some clothes for dinner—a button-down shirt, a pair of jeans—Adam pulled his pants back on and wiped off his belly. The walk there would give him a chance to clear his head before seeing his parents and their friends at this dreaded meal. Indeed, enduring the banality of welcome-home wishes—no matter how well intentioned—was anathema to Adam, and it would take some mental preparation to weather the evening.

Making his way out of the woods behind the house, Adam walked across a meadow interrupted by a two-lane interstate. In the distance, a college baseball field was hosting a game. Adam had played in high school and still took pleasure in remembering how hard he would get in his cup. Sometimes even on the field the sight of his teammates in their grass-stained uniforms was too much for his imagination. As he made his way toward the diamond, it was this thought that drew him closer. Entranced, Adam found a seat on the wooden bleachers and admired its geometry, the predictability of the pitch, the precise constellation of players in their pinstripes. It was order and camaraderie. It was beautiful, dusty nostalgia.

He noticed that the first baseman was looking toward him with too much frequency. After nearly every pitch there was a sly turn of the head, sometimes a tilt of his cap. He wondered if it was a natural curiosity about a new spectator—Adam was one of only a few in the bleachers—or something else behind the player's interest. Maybe twenty-one years old, he had powerful thighs and a solid ass that told of countless sprints between bases. The short sleeves of his jersey exposed forearms built like the bats he swung. Lifting his cap to wipe sweat from his face, he took the opportunity to cast a glance in Adam's direction. Even squinting against the sun, the man's eyes appeared soulful, if such a thing could be gleaned from this distance.

As men in tight uniforms are wont to do in the summer heat, the first baseman reached for his groin to adjust himself. Adam wondered if there was an erection pressing against his cup. He watched intently, struck by the powerful vision of burying his face under the player's balls. Thinking of them brining in the summer sun only made him want it more. It was impossible to avoid now—the cock coming to life in Adam's fatigues. Needing an adjustment now himself, Adam pulled at his waistband and maneuvered his massive tool upward. There was no other choice, and now a full three inches of his cock protruded above his briefs. The nine-incher was not something easy to hide. Subtle as he tried to be, there was no doubt that the guy on the field had taken good notice.

After the last inning, the players assembled to shake hands and murmur "good game." As they took shape in two lines, Adam understood the beauty of uniformity. The men were graceful, effortless as they passed each other; the lines were two perfect forms of ritualized choreography. It reminded Adam of men on the battlefield, losing their self-identities in exchange for a greater purpose. To him there was an ancient knowledge to be learned from a group of men assuming the same physical presentation, all dedicated to a common goal. The vision of it from the bleachers made Adam's balls boil with desire.

When the game ended, the spectators left the stands in search of their sons and boyfriends. But Adam stayed, his erection still aching behind his waistband, scanning the crowd for the first baseman.

There was no one left, and Adam sat alone. In a quiet moment, he admitted to himself that it had all been invented—the sideways glances, the suggestive eyes, the adjustment of the cup. It startled him to accept that none of it had been meant as provocative, but perhaps was some college guy playing baseball in the sun.

Grappling with his realization, Adam descended the steps of the bleachers and followed the perimeter of the field in the direction of the mall. As he passed home plate, he was surprised by a figure leaning against the backside of the dugout. He stopped suddenly, swelling with relief in a deep breath. His stride suddenly confident, he made a direct line to his conquest. Getting closer, he finally made out the face …

It wasn't one that he recognized.

Too late to change course—after all, he was so close he could smell the grime of the game on him—Adam decided there was nothing left to do but introduce himself and pretend this was all intentional.

"It's Adam," he said, holding out his hand, his heart thumping wildly in his chest as he inhaled the smell of the man's sweat. He suddenly wanted nothing more than to get closer, to lick the salt taste off his skin.

"Jeff," the man said.

With locked eyes, they lingered in the strongest handshake.

"Your palm is rough," Adam said. Jeff smiled wide, exposing an unexpected shyness. "Batting practice," he said, squinting in the sun. He had that all-American face seeming to Adam lost in time. Tanned from the summer, with his blue eyes sparkling like ripples of lake water and two days of blond stubble exposing the effortlessness of youth, Jeff was the face of everything pure and honest in the world. After three years in battle, these were things Adam was no longer sure existed. Adam couldn't decide if he wanted to protect or violate them; in truth it was probably both, in equal parts.

"You going or coming back?" Jeff said, his eyes tracing Adam's fatigues.

"Just back."

"And your first priority was my baseball game?"

"Well I was on my way to ..." Adam started explaining and then revised: "Well, it's just"—a pause—"I couldn't wait to fuck you."

Jeff had been watching Adam hungrily from the outfield, mistaking Adam's attention to first base with an interest in him. As the game wrapped up, Jeff hoped he'd be taking this army stud back to his place. But with Adam's comment now hanging in the air, an urgency overwhelmed him. Without a second thought, Jeff dropped his mitt on the ground and fell to his knees. He then unzipped Adam's pants and released the gigantic cock, which was nearly fully engorged. Already hungry for cock, the sight of the monster coming to life made him even more determined to swallow it whole.

Jeff ambitiously dove on the massive thing. But with inches of the shaft left to go, he felt the hard head of the cock hit the back of his throat. Gagging at first, Jeff's throat finally relaxed to allow the inches to enter. Adam turned Jeff's ball cap backwards, making it easier for him to take in the rest of his length. Now with a clear line of sight, he watched the remainder of his shaft slide between the full, wet lips.

Adam felt Jeff's sweat even through the cap on his head. The plains sun was brutal even this late in the day, and it was clear that the devoted sucking was no small effort. The sounds of Jeff's slurping were symphonic to Adam. Although it pained him to interrupt the expert at work, Adam felt an orgasm on the horizon, and there was so much more he wanted from this stud. Grabbing the sides of Jeff's face, Adam forcefully pulled him off his cock and threw him to the ground. He ripped open Jeff's shirt, popping the center-front snaps in one deft movement. What he exposed was a monument to masculinity—a shelf of rock-hard pecs that sat on a broad chest, the taper of the torso to a tiny waist, all of it blanketed by the softest blond hair. At six-foot-one and 190 pounds, Jeff was a powerhouse, but Adam tossed him around with no effort all.

"I hope you don't mind a few more grass stains on these pants," Adam said as he flipped him on his knees, "I intend to rough you up a bit."

"Punishment for losing the game?"

"Trust me, this is a reward, a thank you for welcoming me home."

With that, Adam yanked Jeff's pants to his knees. In front of him was a firm, round ass framed by the two elastic straps of his jock. Jeff tilted his hips and Adam spread him apart, taking in the sight of his perfect form, the slope of his V-shaped back, the muscular forearms, covered in blond fur and dirt, pressed against the ground. Adam spit on the pink pucker, already visible at this angle.

When he leaned forward, Adam breathed in the day's sweat and filth, savoring the pheromone tang before indulging Jeff's rim with his tongue. He was ready to worship this ass, and that worship would necessitate some restraint in the beginning. What Adam wanted was to plunge into the hole, burying his tongue hard and deep, his nose pressed forcefully into the crack of the dude's ass. But he held back, preferring to build suspense by skillfully teasing the perimeter, moving slowly, pulling away and pausing, then torturing the hungry ass by grazing, almost imperceptibly, the bull's-eye with the coiled tip of his tongue.

The protracted moan from below was encouragement for Adam, who started dripping pre-cum at this point, struck by the certainty of how good he could make this guy feel—and just as sure of how much incredible agony he could inflict on his way there. He reached between Jeff's legs and knocked a closed fist against the athletic cup.

"Does it hurt?" he said. "Your hard cock in that cup?"

"Yes," Jeff said, almost whispering. "It's terrible."

Adam responded by using the cup to stroke Jeff's cock. The moans were plaintive now, almost desperate.

Preparing to fuck him, Adam whipped off Jeff's pants, leaving him only in his jock, high socks, and cleats. Adam then picked up the mitt, which was sitting on the grass in arm's reach. "You like the smell of it?" he asked.

"Uh," Jeff said, "Uh-huh. It's grease and dirt and leather and sweat."

"All worn. Years of your sweat in here," Adam said just before he leaned over and forced Jeff's face into the palm of it.

Adam reached for the elastic of his jockstrap and pulled it tight in his fist. With his cock head slick with pre-cum, he pressed it against Jeff's tight ass, meeting the resistance of a hole that had never been fucked.

"Take a deep breath," Adam said.

Jeff inhaled sharply as the first few inches vanished. Adam took his time with the rest, allowing the hole to swallow him slowly, inch by inch. Indeed, this was not a cock to be taken in one gulp by even the most expert ass. As Adam's dark pubes finally met Jeff's ass, it seemed *that* much more of an achievement. The pleading sounds of Jeff's inaugural fuck came first in short grunts. Adam threw the mitt to the side, wanting now to see expressions of pain yield to the most intense pleasure.

As Jeff's ass relaxed around the enormous tool, Adam stepped up the intensity of his assault, little by little, until their fuck was a violent frenzy. The uncontrollable moans were bellowing.

"It's time for the cup to come off," Adam said, reaching around to slip the plastic out of Jeff's jockstrap. Without seeing it, Adam knew that he now had in his possession a giant piece of meat—eight inches at least, thick and throbbing—in his hand.

Adam used the pre-cum he found at the cock head as lube and began stroking Jeff to completion. He knew it wouldn't take long before Jeff was ready, and he had been on the verge himself for many minutes. Pounding this hole for so long without unloading was a feat, and he couldn't resist for much longer.

He was about to tell Jeff to cum when he noticed a man in a base-ball uniform heading toward them.

His heart was pounding hard in his chest—first from the fuck and now from the fear. With his fatigues around his ankles and his cock deep inside Jeff's hole, Adam knew there was nothing to do at this point but take whatever repercussion getting caught would entail. The scare had staved off his orgasm, but he had no intention of dis-banding here without first finishing the job he started.

He said nothing to Jeff and just kept pummeling his incredible ass.

"I'm close," Jeff said, struggling to get the words out.

"Good, so am I," Adam said. "You want to feel me fill you with cum?"

"I want it so bad," Jeff said. "I'm waiting for you. I want to cum with your cum inside me."

Adam's eyes were no longer on Jeff, now focused instead on the man approaching. He was seconds away from spewing a giant load when he recognized him—as the first baseman.

"Wait," Adam said, abruptly letting go of Jeff's cock. "I think we have company." Tortured by the orgasm that had been mere seconds away, he simply waited, questioning whether it would be the anguish of loss returning. Could he possibly feel rejection even with his cock inside another man's ass?

"I want to tag in," the first baseman said as he leaned over, held Adam's face by his stubbly jaw, and kissed him wildly. Adam broke into an insane smile. He was a lunatic doing lunatic things—and being rewarded.

Jeff nodded to his teammate, and then to Adam, who slipped his cock slowly out of the ravaged hole.

The first baseman's shirt and pants were removed and thrown on the ground next to the mitt. He was left, just like Jeff, in a jockstrap, high socks, cleats, and ball cap. Before he got on all fours, he pulled the cup out and let the head of his huge tool leap past the waistband of the jock. Spreading his legs as he knelt, he waited to be abused by the leviathan he instinctively knew was capable of brutality. "Let me have it," he said.

Adam's cock twitched with excitement, but before he started, he reached forward and turned the stud's cap backwards.

Still needing to cum, Jeff got on his knees, held down the waist of the jockstrap, and let his own enormous dick hit the first baseman in the face. "Go ahead, Jack. Take it down."

So Jack, as Adam learned then was his name, opened wide and negotiated the entirety of Jeff's cock to the back of his throat—and beyond. As he choked down the last of Jeff's length, he gurgled and drooled, filled with the heady anticipation of taking it from both sides.

Adam plunged unmercifully into the depths of Jack's hole, holding him still, his giant arms wrapped around his chest. The shock of his size sent quivers through Jack's entire body. Feeling himself inside him, Adam knew it would take nothing to reach orgasm and wanted to make sure Jack would catch up.

As if reading Adam's mind, Jeff mouthed the words "I'm still close."

Adam bucked against Jack's ass, overwhelming him with the intensity that had built over the past hours to culminate in this fantasy.

Their orgasms were a cascade of convulsions, starting with Jeff's, who could not hold back one second longer and filled Jack's mouth with five gushes of his thick cream. Adam held Jeff's eyes as he spewed.

After cumming, Jeff shifted backwards, still on his knees, and tasted himself in Jack's mouth when they kissed. From Adam's vantage point, their faces were completely obscured. All he saw were two backwards caps, the remnants of their uniforms exactly the same. They were mirror images of each other. They were two men losing themselves to a larger purpose, which was about to be realized in an unforgettable orgasm. The warm flood filled him, and Jack lost his own load immediately, his whole body shaking as four thick shots hit the ground.

As the bodies disentangled, a softness came over them. They glowed in the descendant sun. "Holy shit, dude," Jack said, revealing an expansive smile. "Thanks for coming to my game."

"The pleasure is all mine," Adam said.

"I wish there was some way I could repay you."

"It wasn't a chore. You do know that, right?" Looking at his watch, he realized how late it was. "There is something you can do for me," he said.

"Um-hm …?"

"Do either of you have a pair of jeans I can borrow? And a shirt?"

"Yeah," Jack said. "I bet we're the same size. Gotta get it from the locker room."

When he returned with the clothes, Adam said, "Oh, and one more thing?"

They both nodded.

He looked at Jeff. "I'm going to need to take your uniform."

Smiling, Jeff nodded knowingly. "Remember me."

"Of course," Adam said, smelling the uniform pressed against his face. He turned and walked toward his childhood home, his fatigues left on the grass behind him. Sure for the first time in years, he was headed somewhere new.

OUT OF THE BLUE

Rob Rosen

Neither snow nor rain nor heat nor gloom of night stays these couriers from the swift completion of their appointed rounds.

Now *cum,* on the other hand, is another matter entirely. Stickier than snow, slicker than rain, it can certainly slow them down quite a bit—gloom of night or not.

Least that's what I counted on. With Tom, that is. My mailman. My all-man, he-man, fantasy-man, mailman, Tom. Yep, a lot of words for one mail carrier. But Tom, in fact, was a lot of man. A whole hell of a lot, actually.

Picture, if you will, Adonis in blue: pale blue, short sleeved, open-collared shirt, a hint of russet-hued chest hair poking out, biceps bulging at the seams; navy blue shorts, snug in the rump, tree-trunk-thick thighs rammed through, bulge in the front so massive it practically sat in a separate zip code; blue hat resting on waves of auburn; blue sneakers on size twelve feet, or so I imagined—repeatedly; and, lastly, eyes so blue they made the sky pale in comparison, made the sea blush at its inadequacy, the heavens run but a distant second.

Now picture all this, all of Tom, out of the blue, so to speak.

Now therein lay my quandary.

I mean, it was easy enough to get him to my front door, to smile and nod, to hand over an envelope, a box, a package, my finger accidentally/on purpose sliding, gliding across his hair-tinged knuckle, but to get all of this and him out of his uniform … well now, that would take some maneuvering akin to getting the mountain to Mohammed—and the Himalayas at that.

In other words, will meet way. And, yes, that's my name: Will. Go Figure.

"You look hot, Tom," I tried. And talk about your gross understatements. Because the sun looked hot; Tom, you see, outshone even that. "Maybe a nice glass of cold water would help." I looked at my empty hand, minus the stack of mail he'd graciously handed over. "Probably some glasses in the kitchen. Probably some cold water in there as well." *And if I can spill it over your naked body, we'll definitely have the start of a beautiful afternoon,* I thought.

He grinned and winked at me, shooting a bolt of adrenaline down my spine that went *kerpow* inside my crotch. "Not allowed inside, Will." He pointed to the very edge of my house, to where the door would be once I sadly closed it behind him. "That's as far as I can go. Though thanks for the kind offer just the same."

I sighed as I watched him go, gazing longingly at his azure-encased ass as it swung to and fro, calves bulging all the while. "Plan B," I lamented, whishing in fact that I had one.

I stared at his white and blue delivery vehicle, one step above a golf cart, two below an actual car, as it drove away. I then gazed at the boundary from outside to in, to where he'd pointed. It was then that a plan began to formulate. I mean, if I couldn't get him inside, perhaps outside was an option.

After all, I knew his route. Not that I followed him when I thought he wasn't looking, mind you. Though, OK, yes, I did. So sue me. And, again, go figure.

Frantically I waved at the vehicle as it approached, morning sun shining down upon it, casting him in a warm gold. He slowed as he spotted me, head tilted to the side, a grin widening on his supremely handsome face.

"Something the matter, Will?" he asked, his vehicle screeching to a halt.

I'd already pulled some wires and loosened some nuts. In the car. In my head, the nuts had already clearly fallen from the tree. And inside my pants, they were swinging freely. "Car died, Tom," I groused. "Can you help?"

He paused. Clearly, car transmissions didn't exist when the mailman's rain-nor-sleet-nor-hail credo came into being. "I, um … sure, Will. I guess I could take a look," he eventually replied, a resigned sigh detected.

I pointed to the ground. I'd already set a picnic blanket down for him, a fake stain evident beneath the car, à la a well-used bottle of olive oil—extra virgin, of course.

He crouched, the sigh repeated, my crotch throbbing at the sound of it, at the sight of him. On his back he went, legs bent at the knee, spread wide apart, feet planted on the cement, heavenly blue-swathed torso beneath my car. I gulped as I hungrily stared down. There was a gap between meaty thigh and navy fabric. My knees buckled as I ostensibly bent down to admire his progress. In reality, I was admiring the jockstrap beneath his shorts, the faintest hint of crinkled nut-sac revealed. My heartbeat went all jackrabbit-like at the mesmerizing vision.

"You, uh, you doing OK?" I asked, voice trembling, leaning in as close as I dared to, face barely a couple of feet from his bulging mid-section, at his boulder-like calves already slick with perspiration.

"Not seeing anything," he grumbled.

"Really?" I replied. "You sure?" Because a high schooler with remedial shop class could've detected my ministrations.

He pushed himself out. I stood up. Without any undies on, he could clearly see up my shorts, short as said shorts were. His pause returned. His eyes landed on my prize. Three ... two ... one ... *contact*. He gulped and seemed to fight to look away, locking eyes with me instead. So much blue, it was nearly impossible to look away. Suddenly, I knew what a moth felt like when it encountered a flame.

"I've never fixed a car before, Will," he calmly explained.

"But you're so ..." I wanted to say "butch," but went instead with a point to his assortment of muscles. "Well, you know."

He chuckled, the sound like seashells tossed at the shoreline. "Meaning, I can probably *lift* a car, but fix it is another matter entirely." He pushed himself up and stood before me. "Do you have Triple-A?"

I shook my head. I didn't even have AA, and in that instant, anyway, I surely needed a drink. It was then I noticed his greasy hands, a wayward stain on his otherwise pristine sea of blue polyblend cotton. Bingo, I thought. This, after all, was my plan. We'll call it Plan B-minus. Mainly because my car was broke and it would take me a while to fix it once he left. Plus, it wasn't much of a plan really, more like a segue to one.

"You stained your shirt," I croaked out, not waiting for a reply. Instead, I hopped to the rear door of my car, hopped inside, and hopped back a moment later. If it had been Easter, you could've easily pictured me with an assortment of brightly colored eggs, a basket, and some lovely pink ears. Instead, in my hand I held a Tide stick, one of those instant stain removers. "Better take care of it now, before it sets in."

He eyed it, me, and the stain with uncertainty. Seeing as he had a full day ahead of him, minus the time he'd clearly wasted on me, he reluctantly took the stick. "Thanks," he said, starting to administer the Tide to the stain.

"Wait!" I shouted, loud enough to make him, me, and a nearby squirrel jump.

"For what, Will?" he asked, the smile on his face all but vanished.

"You can't use it directly on you," I replied. "The Tide will soak through and bleach your skin."

True? Not a clue. Did it matter? Nope.

He scratched his chin. "You're joking, right?"

I shook my head. "Never about grease stains."

True? Not a clue. Did it matter? Again, nope.

His sigh made its triumphant reappearance. "So, I need to take my shirt off is what you're saying."

My breathing was suddenly ragged. "Afraid so."

He nodded and frowned. And quite suddenly the minus in my B plan had switched to a plus. In other words, his sausage-thick fingers grabbed for the hem of his blue shirt, the eagle aboard quickly taking flight. In more other words, quite suddenly Tom was standing before me shirtless.

I gazed and gaped and gawked. Like a deer caught in the headlights, I was afraid to look away. In fact, my eyes were glued, stapled, and frozen to his magnificent torso, at two pecs like melons, a tuft of hair sprouting between the mounds, trailing down to a six pack with a seemingly extra set of cans, to just the hint of manscaped bush. Michelangelo had never carved anything half as stunning.

He ignored my goggling and gawping, feigning indifference as he went to work on the stain, rubbing it with the picnic blanket I'd handed his way. His pecs bounced as he worked the thankfully smallish blemish. In return, my cock bounced as well. *Down boy,* I thought its way.

"How's it coming?" I asked, voice cracking like a fifteen-year-old boy's.

At the word, *coming,* he momentarily stopped scrubbing and looked up, locking eyes with me once again. My hand trembled, right leg bouncing. "I think we caught it just in time," he replied, holding the shirt up for me to see. "Looks good as new."

I breathed a sigh of relief. Actually, I just breathed. Mainly because I discovered that I'd forgotten to do so while he stood there shirtless. I pointed at the Tide stick. "Good to come prepared."

Again he paused at the word. Again my cock pulsed, throbbed, and promptly bobbed. "Um, yeah." Quickly he got dressed, thanked me again, wished me well with the car, and hot-footed the hell out of there. I think I made the behemoth nervous.

True? Not a clue. Did it matter? Well, of course, nope.

OK, so I'd managed to get my mailman shirtless. Kudos to me. Still, it was a hollow victory. Hollow, that is, once I jacked off behind my dead car. And after I jacked off again once I got home, two hours after I managed to rewire and renut said car—again, kudos to me. Because shirtless was only half the battle; next time I needed the whole kit and caboodle. Mainly because Tom had one mighty fine caboodle and his kit was nothing to sneeze at.

So, yes, Plan B-plus got reworked.

Today I got him at the beginning of his day; tomorrow I'd go for the end, when he wouldn't be in such a rush to get away.

And the mountain didn't go to Mohammed, but the lake sure as hell did.

See, based on my previous excursions—also known as expertly sneaky mailman tailings—Tom's last stop of the day was at the edge of town, at the Peterson residence. Since Clancy Peterson worked nights, this played well in my favor. And since Clancy had a lake off the side of his property, that too played in my favor. Plus, it was warm outside, the summer in full force. In other words, the lake would be warm. So, yeah, what could go wrong?

And, yes, fine, if you want to cue the gloom and doom music, go ahead. I wouldn't blame you.

In any case, I arrived shortly before he did, winding my way around the back roads so that I wouldn't be spotted, and parking behind a shed two blocks over. Mata Hari had nothing on me, stellar spy that I suddenly found myself to be. And then I stripped and made my way to the back of the lake, out of sight to everyone but a couple of curious stray cats.

Naked, cock at half mast, eager for what was about to unfold, I made my way to the lake's edge. I dipped my toe in the water. *Brrr.* And uh-oh. Turned out warm weather didn't necessarily equate to warm lake water. And since it's been working for me thus far: go figure.

Well, in for a penny, in for a pound, I figured. So cock now, OK, *pounding,* I waded in. And though my usually nicely sagging balls did bunch up a bit, my prick remained resolute as it and me treaded to the lake's center, watching, waiting—that is to say, I watched and it waited. Until we no longer had to do so.

"Finally," I exhaled, the delivery vehicle pulling up almost right on time. I inhaled at the sight of Tom, at the beacon of blue, bright smile glinting in the late afternoon sunlight. I then did a backstroke while he finished his work. After that, it was showtime. "Help!" I yelled. "I'm drowning!"

If you already cued the doom and gloom music, now would be a good time to crank it up, seeing as I hadn't accounted for the distance between the center of the lake and the center of Tom. In other words, my shouting promptly fell on deaf ears. I stared as he continued moving away, clearly oblivious to my antics.

"Help!" I shouted, adding a bit of flailing to my repertoire, hoping that the commotion would catch his eye. "Help! I'm drowning!"

Tom got inside his vehicle. My heart sank to my stomach. And my cock, poor thing, miserably shrank. Also, with all my mad flailing, plus the rather chilly temperature of the water, I was developing a bit of a cramp in my leg. "Damn," I said. "That can't be good." Which, yes, was another of those gross understatements.

Tom started to pull away. I started to hyperventilate. And that cramp in my leg spread to fully half of my body. So when I yelled "Help! I'm drowning!" this time I bloody well meant it. *"Help!"* I bellowed, my head barely above the water. *"Help!"* I coughed and sputtered and madly flung my arms.

Lo and behold, the delivery vehicle came to a screeching halt. In that instant, time, though not my thrashing arms, seemed to stand still. I watched through the splash of water as Tom leapt, the blue but a blur now. He spotted me in an instant and, be still my heart—which now, in all likelihood, there was a distinct possibility of actually and irreparably happening—he stripped off his shirt, kicked off his sneakers, and, oh joy, shucked off his navy shorts.

To rephrase all that, the very last thing I'd see on God's green earth was my nearly naked mailman.

Fine, I could live—pardon the expression—with that.

Down I went, my body no longer able to tread, my head following it into the water. I stared up as the rays of the sun shrank and shrank to a pinprick, and then not even that.

Good-bye, cruel world.

I awoke to lips so soft that if felt like I'd landed on a cloud. All things considered, that might have been the case. Then again, I thought not. I popped open my eyes, and there was Tom, his lips on mine.

Hello, supremely fantastic world.

I coughed and spewed out a great deal of water. Tom kept administering mouth to mouth. That is to say, Tom had no choice but to continue administering mouth-to-mouth, seeing as my mouth was now locked to his in a death grip, so to speak. And while I was no longer thrashing, my tongue certainly was.

Gratefully, so was his.

When I finally came up for air, thankful that I could still do so, Tom rolled off of me and onto his back, huffing and puffing all the while.

"What were you doing in the lake, Will?" he managed, in between ragged breaths.

"Swimming?" I tried.

"You sure about that?"

I rolled over onto my side and stared down at him. Well, mostly, I stared at his wet jockstrap, which did *little* to cover his *much*. "Swimming, uh, poorly," I reiterated.

"Better," he quipped, looking my way. "But naked?"

I nodded and instinctively reached across the narrow gap and tweaked his rather fetching nipple. His eyelids fluttered as he moaned, the sound making my cock bounce. "Skinny-dipping poorly then," I replied, tweaking the nipple's twin.

He opened his eyes and stared at me. "What are you doing, Will?"

I paused, then replied, "Um, coming on to you?" I shot him a grin. "Is it working?"

He paused, clearly thinking it over, and replied, "It seems to me there are easier ways to do so."

I continued tweaking, throwing in a tug and a torque for good measure. His jockstrap instantly further bulged. "There are? Really?" *You mean,* I thought, *easier than dismantling my car and faking, then unfaking, a drowning?*

He nodded as he gazed from my eyes to my thick prick, which was aimed his way like a divine divining rod. "You could've just asked me out, you know."

Now he tells me. "OK, want to go out?"

He laughed, that now-familiar chuckle of his riding shotgun down my spine. He then pointed to my tumescence and his growing one. "What, this doesn't count?"

My hand moved from his pert, pink nub of a nipple, slowly traversing his myriad peaks and valleys before landing on the elastic waistband of his wet jockstrap. I lifted the material up and peered inside. His cock sprung out, wide, helmeted head slapping against his belly. Though I was still quite wet, my mouth went Saharan-dry. "Oh, um, this counts, alright," I rasped.

He winked. "Yeah, thought so." He then pointed to the street behind us. "In which case, can we take this show on the road? I mean, a government employee found naked by a lake doesn't exactly make good headlines."

"For the government employee," I interjected.

He touched fingertip to nose, then fingertip to cock. His then mine. After that, he jumped up, grabbed my hand, and hoisted me back to my wobbly legs. With azure uniform in hand, he led me away from the road to the woods behind the lake. Since he was leading me by my rock-solid prick with his other hand, I didn't object.

Once inside the dense copse, he at last turned my way. "Please tell me you didn't plan all this, Will."

I nodded, then shrugged. "I didn't plan all this, Tom."

He smiled and tickled the underside of my chin, and then, at long (long) last, he stripped off his socks and jock and stood there before me, my mailman, naked, erect, and utterly dazzling. "But you did, didn't you?"

My shrug repeated as I stroked his meaty seven inches. His prick throbbed in my grip. "Well, you wouldn't come in for a glass of water."

94

He threw his clothes over a nearby branch and grabbed my prick, both of us jacking away now. "So you opted for an entire lakeful of it?"

I nodded. "Go big or go home, I always say." I stared down at his fifth limb of a dick. "Can't get any bigger than this."

"Point taken."

"Don't mind if I do," I retorted, sinking to my knees.

I slapped his prick against my lips before taking the head in for a swirl. I stared up at his acres of exposed flesh, at his fields of muscle and spray of curly hair that bisected his halves. He stared down, his hands on my head, coaxing his steely cock down my throat. A happy gagging tear streamed down my face as I tickled his hefty balls and hidden, hairy hole.

"*Mmm,*" he hummed. "Feels good."

Which meant that gross understatements traveled in threes.

I popped his prick out of my mouth, however reluctantly, and circled my index finger around his satiny ring. "Could feel better though, you know."

He slapped his prick against one cheek and then the other. "Do tell."

I nodded and kissed the hovering head. "Better yet, I could *show.*"

He took the hint and grabbed his shirt. He turned it inside out. "The stains, I hear, are a bitch to get out," he explained with a knowing wink. He then set the shirt on the ground, crouched down, flipped over, and lay atop it, body outstretched, pole at full-mast. He was now mine. All mine. Oh, how I must've saved a boat-load of kittens in a past life, I thought.

"Legs up, hole out," I commanded. "Special delivery time."

He grinned and did as I'd said, taking his prick in his hand as I crouched down and buried my face in his ass. My mailman's pink, puckered chute tasted like salty lake and musky sweat, like sex and life and a touch of Ivory soap. His balls bounced against the bridge of

95

my nose as I ate him out, my tongue working its way back as far as it would go, my own cock a blur in my sweaty grip.

I retracted my face and gazed down at my progress. His hole was wet with my spit. In other words, good progress. Still, it looked even better with my finger buried to its hilt. Tom's back arched as I wiggled my way to his farthest reaches, his mouth in a pant. When two fingers found their way inside, his moaning amped up a notch. Three, however, was the obvious charm.

"Fuuuck," he exhaled, sharply. He let go of his prick to forestall the inevitable. It swayed and bobbed above his finely-etched belly, balls rocking as I pistoned his ass with my triple digits. "Can two play at this game?" he then added.

I momentarily stopped ramming and cramming and jamming. "I thought two were."

He shook his head. "You thought wrong, Will," he replied. "Now get that ass of yours in my face, please."

I hopped, skipped, and jumped. He didn't have to tell me twice. Or once, really. And so, two seconds later, I was straddling his magnificent frame, his dick stuffed in my mouth, my ass planted firmly against his supple lips.

"Better," I mumbled, in between hungry sucks and slurps on his throbbing tool.

"Much," he agreed, licking and lapping at my proffered hole, tugging on my balls and my prick as he did so.

Again I slid my trio of fingers inside of him, his prick getting worked, my prick also getting worked, one, two, then three of his thick digits finding their way inside of me until the both of us were getting fucked and sucked and plucked with wild abandon. The forest was now silent save for the wild moans and groans of the frenzied animals that suddenly inhabited it.

Eventually, I thought to ask, "Hey, um, Tom, mind if I ask you a favor?"

96

He stopped slurping and tugging. "Hey, um, Will, sure, I can try four fingers."

I laughed. "No, not that."

"Darn."

My laugh repeated itself. "I mean, you can fuck me with four fingers if you like. Hell, make it a happy family of five, for all I care. But that's not the favor."

He spanked my ass, left cheek then right, the sound pinging between the trees. "Then shoot."

"I intend to," I replied. "Though preferably with you wearing your post office hat."

"Dirty boy," he chided.

I rolled off of him. "Yeah, I think we already knew that." I looked at him expectantly. "Well?"

He smiled, broadly, and rose to his feet, cock swaying like a billy club, muscles rippling. "I can do one better," he replied, turning his shirt right-side-in before slipping it back on, the hat sitting firmly on his head a moment later. "This more to your liking?"

I groaned at the sight of him, of my mailman, half-dressed, fully erect, so beautiful as to take your very breath away. "Simply icing on the cake, Tom," I replied.

He jacked his prick. "And speaking of icing."

I closed the gap between us, our lips again joined as one, copious amounts of spit quickly swapped. I gazed up at his hat and down at his shirt. All in all, even with the near-drowning, all was now perfect. And so with both pricks again getting furiously jacked and both holes getting fervently worked, Tom and I worked the cum up from each other's heavy balls.

"Close," he soon grunted.

"Closer," I then groaned.

And with his hole clenched around my fingers, his mammoth cock shot an equally mammoth load, drenching my belly with a veritable river of aromatic spunk. At the sight of this, at the smell and sound, my own cock erupted, spewing a torrent of cum out and down, all of it dripping off his hairy thigh and onto the forest floor below.

The kiss was repeated, softer, slower this time, our hands retracted from asses and pricks, our bodies melding together as one.

"Messy," he whispered into my mouth.

I chuckled. "Luckily, there's a giant bathtub a short walk away."

His chuckle mirrored my own. "They say that more people drown in their bathtubs each year than die in plane crashes."

I grimaced. "Been there, done that."

And did it matter? Did I care about risking life and limb one again as we strode hand-in-hand into the chilly water? Oh, hell to the no.

True? Not a clue. Did it matter? Last and final time, nope.

INTO THE ORANGE

Mike Connor

The darkroom of the Pistol, a video bar on Old Warm Springs Road wasn't doing much for Jasper tonight. Scanning the room, he saw the same twenty-odd guys who were always there—the usual pick-up-driving good old boys who were fixtures at this, one of only four gay bars in Muscogee County. Most of them had already enjoyed Jasper's big dick in their mouths, asses, or both.

His evening had begun around ten thirty. At home in front of the TV, he'd had nothing stimulating going on. Just a quiet night of Coors beer and a mindless reality show on TLC. But he'd kept shifting in his chair, uncomfortable. His cock wouldn't go down. It had been hard all day, and by a quarter past ten he'd realized that if he didn't do something about it, he wouldn't get any sleep.

His tool was a thing of beauty. The massive size and perfect shape had made every trick he'd ever had gasp the first time they saw it. But Jasper's cock was like a nagging boyfriend who made his life miserable when it wasn't satisfied. All it wanted was pleasure, and getting there wasn't always easy. Especially when he had to drive fifteen miles from the boondocks of Phenix City across the Chattahoochee River into downtown Columbus just to get laid. Oh sure, Jasper could jerk himself off—but he knew from experience that wouldn't be enough. This was one of *those* boners—the kind that needed something special. And that something special obviously wasn't in the darkroom at the Pistol.

It wasn't that the eager, open-mouthed guy currently between his legs wasn't doing a good job. He was a fine cocksucker, giving it his best shot—and getting more of Jasper's meat down his throat than most guys could. But there was something missing. Something Jasper couldn't put his finger on.

He hadn't even seen the guy's face. He'd hit the backroom after two beers. He never had more when he was driving, and besides, there were only so many Beyoncé videos he could take while dealing with such a painful hard-on. So down the hall, past the bathrooms Jasper went, through the dark velvet curtains that led to the anything-goes dark den of debauchery in back.

The room was nearly pitch black, but Jasper could make out shapes and occasionally faces, whenever someone parted the curtains. Heading to his favorite corner in the back, he'd navigated with his hands, managing a couple gropey-gropes along the way. A cock here, a firm ass there, even something sticky—which he'd immediately rubbed on the corduroy shirt of the next person he passed. Then, just as he'd reached his spot, he'd felt hands on his crotch. At first it seemed totally random but once it settled on the growing denim-covered bulge, the focus immediately shifted, became very single-minded.

The top of his jeans had been quickly snapped open and then *pop, pop, pop* —came the parting of his button-fly. For a split second, he'd felt a hand on each side of his waist as the Levi's were yanked down to his ankles. This was followed by the sensation of both hands cupping the waistband of his snug-fitting Andrew Christian briefs, which were similarly gotten out of the way. Jasper never went commando. He

100

disliked the feeling of his junk hanging willy-nilly down the leg of his jeans. It usually felt cramped or squashed, especially when his jeans were tight. And with the size of his tool, Jasper needed the support.

Besides, his package looked really good in briefs. Especially when his snake was uncoiled, thick, and eager to shoot its venom, as it was at this particular second. Of course, the stranger on his knees wasn't able to see any of this, but the curious, cock-hungry redneck was more than making up for the lack of light with his sense of touch. Every inch of Jasper's meat was being explored by the man's fingers: each vein, every ridge, from the pinkish head, down the wide shaft, all the way to his balls.

Lips—and a throat—enveloped Jasper's cock, warm and welcoming. How intensely erotic, pushing his member into a new mouth, not to mention the dirty thrill of getting sucked off by someone you couldn't see. Enjoying the sensation, Jasper grabbed the back of the guy's head as a way of goading on the action. His fingertips felt a bristly crew cut, common in this neck of the woods. The scratchy, short hairs sent an electric thrill from his palms up his arms. Pulling the man's head closer to him, he forced more of his rod down the eager cocksucker's throat.

He imagined that the guy swallowing him was blond, six feet tall, and clean-shaven. This was his fantasy man, the one he jerked off to on the rare nights his cock would settle for self-love. He knew that wouldn't be the case tonight. Nope. Tonight, he grumbled to himself for the umpteenth time, he'd have to find something special or he wouldn't be sleeping at all. And it was quickly becoming clear, despite the skill of the mouth sliding up and down his grateful rod, that something special wasn't going to be found here.

Though Jasper didn't dare light up the display on his digital watch, he thought it was about eleven forty-five, maybe even midnight. He could still hear Beyoncé from the Pistol's main room. She was

101

demanding over and over that someone to put a ring on it, which was bad enough in the radio version, let alone in a twelve-minute remix. She went on and on and on. *Cheese and rice,* he thought with annoyance, *write some more goddam lyrics already!*

"What'd you say?" The mouth let go of his cock. Now words were coming from it. "Write what?"

Hells bells! Sometimes in the heat of the moment, Jasper accidentally thought out loud. Which was super awkward. "Don't stop," he said—on purpose this time. "That felt so good."

Time to finish this and move on.

The stranger tongued Jasper's cock head, and before long his mouth was back in action too. The stranger's hand slid up and down the massive spit-soaked shaft in perfect unison with his lips. Even in the dark, Jasper could tell it was a small hand—it didn't reach all the way around his hearty tree trunk—but it was doing the trick.

"Gah," he moaned, feeling the jizz building up in his nuts and begging to be set free. *"Fuck,* I'm cumming!"

He expected the stranger to pull his mouth away but he didn't, so Jasper showered the warm throat with his hot load, then quickly pulled the guy up for a kiss. He wanted to sample as much of his own seed as he could before the guy gulped it down. Now face-to-face, his tongue forced its way into the cocksucker's mouth, spelunking for the savory taste of his own slimy happiness.

When the darkroom's velvet curtains parted in the middle of their make-out session, Jasper was able to get a look at the recipient of his milky-white gift. The guy was *not* blond, six feet tall, or even cute, which instantly killed his fantasy. But just as Jasper pulled away, ready to bail, the stranger reached for his hand and pulled it to his own crotch. Through the satiny fabric of athletic shorts Jasper felt a boner going on, but nothing to write home about. Certainly nothing worth playing with.

Especially on a night like this, when he was so hot his skin felt like Georgia asphalt in the noonday sun.

"Gotta go," Jasper whispered into the under-endowed guy's ear. "Thanks for the, uh *sucky-suck,* bub."

His guess about the time had been way off. Either that darkroom blow job had been really good or it had been a *sixty*-minute version of "Single Ladies" he'd suffered through. However it had been, now the clock said 1:00 a.m. His dick was still hard and demanding more. The bars were closing soon, so Jasper headed toward South Lumpkin Park.

High above the makeshift parking space where Jasper left his red Ford F-150 was a failing streetlight. It flickered on and off, making a buzzing sound every time it changed, and Jasper hoped this was a sign that ultimate sexual satisfaction was just around the corner. Or bush. Or magnolia tree. Or on the swing set.

But there were surprisingly few guys milling about in the park—or lurking, as Jasper usually thought of the slow, furtive movements of horned up men on the prowl for a quick fuck or suck. Because of his superior equipment, Jasper usually ended up with his pick of the available orifices. All he had to do was park himself someplace well lit, pull out his hard cock, and start stroking it. Like a moth to a bug light, the men would come.

One night a couple years back, Jasper had found himself in the center of a circle of about eight guys, all of them salivating like dogs over his massive bone. After quickly surveying the boys, he'd made his choice—the six-foot tall blond, of course—which he'd shown by simply pointing his finger. Summoned, the shirtless stud had eagerly made his way over and bowed before the altar of Jasper's divining rod.

"Open your mouth," Jasper had told him. Sometimes he got off on being bossy. "Suck my cock."

To the envy of the circle's non-chosen ones, the stud had expertly swallowed his rock-hard tool. Blondie had put on an amazingly hot show for the onlookers that night, his hands all over Jasper's body, traveling up to pinch his nipples, wandering around back to graze the smooth skin of his ass and play with his hole.

That night had been still and sultry like this one, one of those nights where the heat lay on his skin like a wet, hot bath towel. One of those nights Jasper's boner just wouldn't quit nagging him. He quickly took advantage of the situation. After shooting his first load all over the blond stud's hungry face, he'd scanned the bystanders and found the second hottest banana in the bunch. Again, he summoned him with only a *come here* gesture of his index finger.

"Eat my ass," Jasper had grunted to guy number two, who wasted no time in obeying. Using both hands to spread Jasper's firm cheeks, the man's tongue sampled his hole. *Jesusfuck you taste amazing,* he'd breathed so that Jasper could hear him in between sloppy slurps. He was an expert ass licker, and each tongue lashing sent waves of pleasure through Jasper's body. He was still hard, of course, and couldn't wait to cum again—which he knew would happen soon just from getting his salad tossed.

That night he'd been the prince of the park. Jasper had ended up summoning the rest of the masturbating onlookers, one by one, *Price Is Right*-style. "Come on down!" his index finger told them all. "You're the next contestant on *Get Jasper's Rocks Off!*"

Within minutes, Jasper was being devoured from every angle like Sebastian Venable—only in a good way. He was sucked, licked, cupped, fingered, eaten out, and rubbed in all his hot spots—and those late night perverts who didn't have access to an erotic body part were content to merely stroke his muscular back, his sinewy forearms, or lick his work-hardened thighs. Anything to be part of this unplanned park orgy, this shared worship of a hillbilly Greek god with an enormous cock and the stones to shamelessly demand such attention.

It was like being the leader of a sex cult—the head rush this feeling of power brought him was that intense. Three of the guys had turned out to be aggressive bottoms, so Jasper had lined them up on a stone wall, three cock-loving ducks in a row. He went from ass to ass, teasing them at first by rubbing his swollen cock head against each begging hole, then slowly sliding himself in. The first few times he'd gone only as far as his cock's swollen, fleshy knob, in spite of desperate pleas from the men to shove it all the way in. *One, two, three,* he'd gone. *Knob, knob, knob.* This was his way of priming their holes for what he knew would be a far more intense experience than any of them had hoped for. Guys were usually brave—cocky, even—when it came to taking Jasper's manhood, but most of them weren't ready for how deep he could actually go with it.

These guys were no exception. After several rounds of *one-two-three* teasing with just the tip, Jasper had surprised the guy in the middle by shoving his ten-and-a-half incher all the way in. Caught completely off guard, the guy had screamed like a girl. Secretly pleased but not wanting to torture him, Jasper had pulled out and then moved on to the next duck, whose insides had gotten a similar shock. Soon, all three guys were enjoying a few full-in-and-out pumps at a time while their mouths kept the hangers-on happy by taking two or three cocks each in turn.

Pumping load after load down throats, onto faces, and into now cavernous assholes, it was one of those rare nights Jasper had felt truly *satisfied.* One of those nights that, despite the inadequate A/C in his trailer, he'd actually gotten to sleep—and slept *well.*

Unfortunately, that wasn't happening in Lumpkin Park tonight. None of the lurkers appealed to Jasper. Not wanting to waste time like he had at the Pistol, he walked back to his truck, where he noticed the buzzing streetlight had gone out completely.

He took that as a sign he'd made right call.

He took 185 to the Airport Thruway, going over the speed limit the whole way, with his truck windows down. The humid breeze did nothing to ease the ungodly itch just beneath the surface of his skin. He knew just where he was headed. For some reason, the Home Depot off of Britt David Road was open twenty-four hours a day. Guess it was common for somebody to need a good pipe fitting at three in the morning. Or some hot caulk. He laughed at his own desperate wit, stroking himself through his jeans as he mashed the gas pedal with one work-booted foot.

Jasper, on the other hand, was desperate for a screw. And this was his last chance. He'd gotten lucky at the Homo Depot, as he liked to think of it, a couple times before. So either this worked, or he'd have no choice but to forget about sleep and take his unsatisfied early morning wood to breakfast at the Denny's out on Macon Road, where he might find a geriatric fag to give him a hand job in the dirty men's room that smelled of urinal cakes.

The gigantic store, all tall ceilings, cold stale air, and warehouse echoes, was virtually empty. The pickings were sure to be slim, Jasper thought with grim determination. Still, he was here, so he might as well give it a shot. He was single and ready to mingle. A man on a mission, trolling the DIY mecca with his own internal stud finder, desperate for a nice, long hose to match his own.

Seeing no one on the floor, not even at one of the checkouts, Jasper glanced up. High above aisle sixteen, which was marked HARDWARE, the sign promised the following items: oil, grease, rope, hammers, nails, and something called "tie downs."

Thinking this was as good a sign as any, he headed that direction.

106

Turning the corner into the aisle, the first thing he saw was a six-foot blond Adonis. *Yeah! Now we're in business,* Jasper thought. The man wore tight blue jeans, faded within an inch of their life, and a tight fitting green T-shirt that showed off every sickeningly sculpted muscle in his arms and torso. From the side, Jasper saw perky nipples poking through the nearly sheer fabric up north, and further south, the Jon Hamm-worthy bulge of his crotch. Jasper licked his lips at the sight, breathed a sigh of relief. The first time he'd seen this kind of perfection in Muscogee County. The guy looked like he'd stepped out of a Taylor Swift video. Abso-fuckin-lutely amazing.

Then an equally perfect looking woman joined him, just walked up and put her arm around his waist.

Quickly backtracking, Jasper fled aisle sixteen. Practically running, he turned the corner and—*bam!*—ran directly into something big, burly—

—And orange. It was the last thing he saw before he hit the floor.

"Hey bro, you OK?

The first thing Jasper saw when he came to was a field of orange. The first thing he felt was that nagging boner, once again begging to be freed from the prison of his Levi's and satisfied with something special.

A burly man leaned over Jasper, wearing a look of concern. He had an adorable face, big brown eyes, a sexy, blunt oversized nose, and full lips. His skin was olive, his hair a barely-under-control mass of thick black curls. Super-hot guy, thought Jasper, looked like maybe he was part Spanish or Italian. The way the orange Home Depot apron clung to his stocky frame made Jasper's prick throb. Under the store logo were the words "HELLO, MY NAME IS …" followed by a hand-scrawled SEAN, in big, childlike letters. So cute. *So* fucking sexy.

From either side of that orange apron, brawny arms awkwardly

107

tried to pull Jasper up off the concrete floor. Unsurprisingly, they were alone. No blond Adonis anywhere in sight. Where was he, anyway—in the power tool section, drilling his perfect girlfriend?

"Can you stand?" The orange was talking again. Sean. Not the type Jasper usually went for, yet so fucking adorable in that apron. This was a first—Jasper had never before been turned on by wardrobe—but he suddenly felt a gob of moist goodness in his briefs. "Can you hear me?" His voice was soft, concerned, with no middle Georgia twang. A newcomer?

Jasper smiled. "I can hear you." He wanted to say, *I can do more than* that *if you let me,* but thought better.

The guy put his hairy arms around Jasper and swept him to his feet. Pretending it was an embrace, Jasper pushed his throbbing cock ever so slightly against the front of that apron. It gave him an electric thrill. More pre-cum leaked from his cock.

"Sure you're OK?" Sean asked.

Jasper watched his hands, wondered what else on him was big. "I'm fine." *You really know how to knock a guy off his feet.*

Sean chuckled. "Very funny."

Gah! Had Jasper accidentally thought out loud again?

"Glad you're not hurt. Can I uh, help you with anything?" he asked awkwardly.

Jasper wondered whether the chest under that orange apron was covered in the same black hair that grew on those burly arms. *Fuck yeah, baby. You can seed me.*

The burly man smiled. "The garden section's this way …"

Shit.

The stud in orange started toward the store's east end, past the empty checkout stations and patio furniture. Jasper followed, silently commanding his brain to stop thinking, his eager cock leading the way as he took in those broad shoulders, the curve of Sean's bubble butt.

108

By the time they reached the garden section, Jasper—who usually stood back and let men come to *him*—was desperate. His nagging boner demanded he make a move.

"I don't normally work in this section," said Sean, "but if you tell me what you're into I'll do my best."

I'm into you, Jasper heard himself say, though he wasn't sure if it was in his head or out loud. His eyes were still fixated on the apron.

After an awkward pause, Sean cleared his throat. "I'm, uh … guessing you really like plants."

"What makes you say that?" Jasper said, wishing Sean would plant one on him.

The burly man pointed to the bulge in Jasper's 501s. The head of his cock was plainly visible through the denim—it was that hard. "You seem pretty excited."

Jasper smiled. "Ain't got nothing to do with plants."

"Really. What's it about then?"

"You." *And the apron.*

Crickets. Deafening silence. Had he gone too far? Would Sean call security and have him ejected from the premises? With those jacked arms of his, he didn't need security. God, Jasper really wanted this stud in the orange apron.

An adorably sly smile spread over Sean's face.

"Why are you smiling?" Jasper asked.

"Thinking of our store's motto: '*You Can Do It—With Our Help.*'"

Wanting more than anything to *do it,* Jasper pressed his mouth against the sexy, full lips. Damn, what a kiss—ravenous, insatiable. If Sean's mouth tasted this amazing, thought Jasper, how would his spunk taste? He couldn't wait to find out.

He wasted no time dropping to his knees, diving underneath the orange apron, and pulling down Sean's zipper. In one quick motion, he unleashed an impressive eight-inch uncut monster that looked good enough to eat. Leaning in for a whiff, Jasper inhaled deeply, his head spinning with the delicious aroma of the man's cock and balls.

With the tip of his tongue, Jasper licked the underside of Sean's shaft. Then he carefully pushed the veined rod down so he could taste the top. As he licked downward, he lightly grazed the swollen head, drawing an audible gasp.

"You like that?" Jasper asked from underneath the apron.

"Fuck yeah, man."

Jasper grunted, opening his mouth wide. He drooled as he finally wrapped his lips around the burly man's slab of hooded meat. Quickly, he swallowed it whole, his mouth taking the entire length to the back of his throat in one swift move. As he buried his face in Sean's untrimmed bush, he felt sticky salty pre-cum coating the back of his throat. Easing off a little, he wrapped his fist around the base of the shaft and pulled back the man's foreskin to get a good look at the head, now throbbing and a purplish color.

The thick tool swelled in Jasper's hand. Taking it again in his mouth, he pumped up and down the length as he sucked, provoking deep moans and copious leaking of Sean's salty juices. Releasing the beast altogether, Jasper watched as a string of pre-cum stretched from his lips to the tip of the burly man's cock before it snapped and disappeared.

"Want you to fuck my mouth," he said, looking up and seeing only orange, "and I don't want you to be gentle—"

Through the apron, Sean grabbed the back of Jasper's head and held it in place as he ferociously slammed his tool back into the hungry piehole. He pumped in rhythm, driving his fuck-stick in and out of Jasper's lips at a wild, urgent pace. After a few quick thrusts, his big hands yanked Jasper's head all the way toward him, impaling the cocksucker and practically choking him. Hearing no complaints, he continued the savage face-fuck at close range until Jasper, needing to breathe, abruptly pushed him off and stood.

With something else on his mind, something new, Jasper unbuttoned his jeans and yanked them down, taking his Andrew Christians with them. He tore off his Camp David tee and tossed it carelessly aside. Completely naked and exposed in the garden section, with its greenhouse ceiling giving a view of the night sky above, he turned around, grabbed a shelf that held some sort of small prickly plants, and stuck his ass in Sean's direction.

"Fuck me," he said insistently, unable to remember the last time he'd wanted something so badly.

Stepping toward him, Sean bent down, spread Jasper's cheeks, and spit in his hole. Reaching up, he stuck two of his thick fingers into Jasper's mouth. "Need more spit," he said, sliding his digits in and out.

Jasper took a moment to enjoy the earthy taste of Sean's calloused fingers while coating them with his saliva. Reluctantly, his lips let go, then Sean's hand returned to Jasper's ass. Slowly, teasingly, he eased in one finger, then two. When a third finger joined the others, Jasper let go a moan that even he could hear fell somewhere between pain and pleasure. What was this feeling, this bottomless need? He'd never been fucked before, had thought he couldn't even imagine doing it, and certainly wasn't about to reveal that now. But he *had* to have this stud inside him—otherwise he might never sleep again.

Jeans around his hips, work "uniform" still hanging from his neck, Sean raised the orange apron in order to free his throbbing eight-incher. He tapped it provocatively against Jasper's twitching entrance, then slowly invited himself in.

Whoa! Jasper stifled a gasp as Sean pushed the head of his cock home. His hole stretched as the thick rod pressed in, deeper and deeper, each inch threatening to tear soft flesh. How could something so painful be so welcome? Jasper wondered. He took a deep

111

breath and relaxed—just as he'd instructed many a bottom to do—then eased back towards Sean's hips.

Another deep breath. "Go as far as you can," he demanded. "Wanna feel your balls against my ass."

To Jasper's delight, Sean did as he'd been told. By the time he was in all the way to his pubes, it was clear the burly man knew what he was doing. The massive member that seconds earlier had literally threatened to tear Jasper apart now felt like it belonged there, and would always be welcome. Balls deep, Sean hesitated for a few seconds, then the thrusting began, gently at first. His sturdy cock found the rhythm, and Sean began pounding Jasper's eager hole. Tauntingly, brawny Sean pulled his rod almost all the way out. Swiveling his hips, he plunged it back in.

From all over Jasper's body, the tingling began. He'd felt nothing like it since the first time someone else's hands had gone down the front of his pants, looking for the Holy Grail of his cock. Speaking of cocks, Sean's was hitting the spot—*that* spot, the one Jasper had only ever heard about, along with shouts of "*Jesus!*" and "*Motherfucker!*" when he was hitting it in another guy's ass. His knees went weak with the sensation—God it felt so fucking good! Even the few times he'd let someone finger his ass while blowing him, he'd never been able to imagine this. Now he understood it completely, but still it wasn't enough.

"Fuck me hard!" Jasper shouted, not caring who might see or hear.

Sean rammed deeper into him, pushing him forward—his brawny chest forcing Jasper into the metal shelving of the store's garden section. Jasper pushed back, matching him stroke for stroke, moan for moan, thrust for thrust. He imagined his hole opening like the maw of a predator, devouring Sean's thick rod as it filled him. Pain was present too, insistent, with delight—threatening to become everything he knew.

Sean shivered, his breath hitched. Jasper knew he was getting close, wanted every drop of him.

"Cum in my ass," Jasper begged. "Fill me up."

With a primal wail, Sean fired into Jasper's hungry ass, coating his insides with warm cream. Grunting with the intensity, after several more hard thrusts, Sean relaxed—collapsed, really—against Jasper, who reached back, grabbing at Sean's beefy cakes to pull him closer.

"Don't pull out," he growled. "Wanna feel you inside me when I cum."

Cream churning in his nuts, Jasper stroked his painfully swollen pud. Groaning loudly—almost crying with mingled pain and plea-sure—he let loose a massive round of jizz all over a row of succulents. The poor plants never saw it coming. Jasper's toes curled, his eyes squeezed shut with the force of his orgasm.

Sean leaned forward, his half-hard cock still prodding the inside of Jasper's ass. He gripped the shelving unit with one hand, using the fingers of his other hand to scoop the pooling creaminess of Jasper's cum from the shelf. Bringing fingers to his mouth, he sampled it, softly moaning his appreciation. Obviously the burly man loved the taste of Jasper's cum as much as Jasper did.

Well, that was a surprise, Jasper thought, letting Sean's softening member pop out of him. Hells bells, he felt ravaged, but in a good way. He turned, looking look into Sean's dark eyes. Who was this man in the orange apron who'd turned him inside out? All night he'd been on the prowl for something special—but he'd found something *amazing.* Something he wasn't sure he'd ever want to give it up.

"Wow, you give great customer service," Jasper said, changing the subject in his head so as not to reveal it. "What time do you get off?"

Sean laughed. "Think I just did."

"No, I mean—what time do you get off work?"

"My shift ended at three thirty."

Jasper looked at his watch. Three thirty-five. *Excellent.* "You wanna come over?"

"Love to," Sean said, barely able to conceal a smile as he took off his work apron. "Just give me a second to drop this in back—"

"No, *bring it!*" Jasper said, surprised by the urgency in his own voice. "I mean I'd … I'd *like* you to bring it."

"Why?"

"Not sure." Jasper smiled in spite of himself. "For some reason, I'm just really into the orange."

"OK." Sean shrugged, then muttered. "Whatever, bro."

Hmm, Jasper mused with a little smile—sounded like sometimes Sean let his thoughts slip out too.

Leaving the store, Jasper knew he definitely wouldn't be getting *any* sleep tonight—except now, that was a really good thing.

BEAR WITH ME

Landon Dixon

Roderick Justus trooped into the log structure that served as the RCMP command post in Dawson City, snapped his right hand up to the stiffened flat brim of his felt campaign hat and bellowed, "Constable Roderick Justus, sir! Reporting for duty!"

Corporal Neilson glanced up from the piece of paper he'd been studying, looked at the clean-shaven, prim and proper officer in his scarlet serge tunic, midnight blue breeches with yellow stripes down the sides, gleaming Sam Browne leather belt, and shiny oxblood riding boots. "At ease," he commented dryly. "This isn't the parade ground back in Regina. It's the Yukon Territory."

"Class of '22! Yes, sir!" Justus shouted, proud of his recent graduation from the training academy in Saskatchewan. He snapped his arm back down to his side, then clasped his brown-gloved hands behind his back and planted his feet wider apart.

"We wouldn't have called you up from Edmonton, constable," Neilson stated, "if we weren't desperately shorthanded at the moment."

The blond-haired rookie blinked his big blue eyes. His button nose twitched.

"It's a rough life up here, Justus, and we normally only take men with some experience under their belts. We cover a territory almost as vast and rugged as Alaska, with only a twenty-man detachment." Neilson twirled the ends of his dark mustache. "But most of the miners, trappers, and mountain men are in town for the winter now, or camped out along the Yukon and Klondike Rivers on the outskirts, and we've got our hands full." The corporal handed the sheet of paper he'd been examining to the constable. "This man is Ferdinand 'Fer' Peltier."

Justus looked at the headshot of the clean-shaven, bald-headed man, noted the typed statistics of the man's immense height and weight with a cocked blond eyebrow.

"He's a prospector and trapper, used to be partnered with a local gambler and all-around ne'er-do-well, Earnest Rigby. Rigby was found in Paradise Alley behind the Gold Dust Saloon two days ago, knocked out and now in a coma. Peltier was seen leaving the scene on the night in question. The two men had had a public falling out six months previously. Your job is to find Fer Peltier and bring him back to Dawson to face justice."

The constable shifted uneasily. "Um, did the witness say what direction Peltier was headed in?"

"Yes. North."

Corporal Neilson looked back down at the papers on his rough-hewn pine desk. "A local guide, Thomas Cook, is standing by with a couple of dog teams out back. Good luck, Justus."

Constable Justus snapped his boots together and squared up, whipped his right arm up in a parting salute, then wheeled about and marched out of the command post—the perfect picture of the newly-minted Royal Canadian Mounted Police officer. And the rawest of recruits and naivest of men to the ways and wiles of the brutally harsh land of the Yukon Territory.

The sun was a wan yellow disk hanging low in the bright blue sky, it being early January. The air was so cold and crisp it almost broke off in Justus's mouth and choked him as he crunched through the brittle white snow around to the back of the log command post.

Thomas Cook was waiting with a pair of sleds, a team of eight dogs harnessed to each sled two abreast. The fur-wrapped, bushy-bearded guide regarded the great-coated constable with a mixture of contempt and pity. He took a slug of whiskey from the pewter flask he kept in his parka, tore off a plug of black tobacco with his teeth and worked it around in his steaming mouth. And then he showed Justus the rudimentary ropes on handling his dog sled team.

They headed out of town on the snow-packed trail leading north through low hills of stunted pine forest and thick bush. And five miles down the trail, after numerous plunges and back-flips into the three-foot-high snowbanks that bordered the winding route, Justus felt he was starting to get the hang of running his dog team. Let the animals do the hard work of pulling; just stand on the sled runners and hang onto the handles and call out the occasional "Mush!" with a crack of the whip whenever the dogs threatened to get bogged down or entangled.

They made good progress on the trail of Fer Peltier, cutting through the crystallized cold air.

"He's probably headed for his dugout on Foam Lake," Cook stated, when they finally took a break to rest the dogs and snack on some beef jerky. "If he isn't already holed up there. He moves fast through the bush."

Cook pressed a fur mitten to each of his frosted nostrils and snorted in turn, then gulped a large mouthful of whiskey out of his flask. His breath blew white clouds, almost one-hundred proof. "Peltier and Rigby used to be partners, you know, in more ways than one." He winked an iced eyelash as he bit off a chaw.

Justus stared at the snow-crusted beard of the squarely-built man. "Oh, yes," he stated tersely, adjusting his RCMP-issue fur cap with the ear flaps, with his RCMP-issue brown gauntlets. He felt he had to keep up appearances, and standards, even out in the wilds.

Cook spat out a stream of black juice onto the back of a hunkered-down husky, making it yelp. "Yes. Paradise Alley is for lovers, you know." He pumped a tobacco-yellowed digit in between the circled stubby thumb and forefinger of his other hairy hand. "Maybe they were trying to patch things up, if you know what I mean, but things got out of hand."

"Shall we get going?" Constable Justus said briskly.

Cook nodded, sliding his mittens back on. "The men moiling for gold do strange things up here in the land of the midnight sun."

They were forty miles further down the trail, the sun beginning to sink beneath the hilled horizon, Thomas Cook good and drunk and weaving from side-to-side on the back of his sled, Constable Justus's boyish face the same shade of deepening blue as the sky, when the dogs of both teams suddenly skidded wildly to a stop in a furry pile-up and started howling.

Cook jumped off his sled just in time and landed in a snowbank. Justus was flung over the top of his sled by the abrupt stoppage and landed on the hindquarters of a pair of balled-up, barking huskies.

Cook climbed to his feet and stumbled forward. He studied the snow trail just beyond where the dogs had put on the breaks. "Gall almighty!" the man frothed, stone-cold sober all at once.

He grabbed the harness of his two lead dogs and bodily swung the huskies around on the trail. The other six dogs scrambled to follow suit, until Cook's sled was pointed due south. The man jumped on the runners and urgently mushed.

"Where are you going!? What's wrong!?" Justus yelled, running alongside the retreating guide and his dog team.

"Grizzly bear tracks!" Cook shouted back. "Fresh ones! Lots of them! I've got a thing about grizzly bears! And they've got a thing about me! Bad medicine, pilgrim! My trail ends here!"

Constable Justus grabbed onto the man's arm, floundering down the path to keep up. "But we've got guns! You can't just run away! We have a duty—"

Cook tore his arm loose and shoved Justus away. The constable went tumbling into the thick brush alongside the trail.

He sat on his haunches deep in the snow, and watched his guide swing around a corner of the trail and disappear from sight. Just as a loud roar sounded even above the dogs' high-pitched yelping.

Justus swung his head around. Two huge grizzly bears lumbered out of the bush and onto the trail ten yards away from where he squatted in the snow. The constable's eyes popped. He jumped to his feet. The bears rose up on their hind legs and roared again, towering five feet and fourteen hundred combined pounds above the small upholder of laws in the Yukon Territory. The man's sled, with his .50 rifle on board, raced away up ahead on the trail, pulled by eight straining huskies.

"Easy now!" Justus gulped, backing away from the pair of enormous bears, fumbling under his coat for his service revolver in its leather holster.

The grizzlies weren't listening to reason, however, or respective of the rule of man's law. They thumped their huge front paws back down on the trail, sending up clouds of loose snow. Then they lowered their massive heads and charged Justus. Mammoth brown mounds of muscle with four-inch-long sharp claws.

Justus desperately backpedaled, tripped, fell flat on his back in the snow. The bears galloped towards him, their thick fur rippling with power. They were five yards away from the fallen constable and closing at terrifying speed when a rifle shot rang out, a bullet blasting across the wet, black snouts of the two charging bears.

119

The giant grizzlies skidded to a stop and lifted their heads and sniffed at the air. Another heavy caliber shot boomed out, this well-aimed bullet creasing the fur on the bears' sloping foreheads. They yowled and scampered off into the bush on either side of the stunned, frozen-in-fear constable.

"They're real mean when they haven't found a den for the winter yet," a voice sounded nearby.

Justus jerked his head to the right and looked up at the great bear of a man who had stepped out of the bush and onto the trail. He was gripping a rifle in his two enormous hands, his body covered in fur and his face in hair.

The rookie RCMP officer was so relieved and grateful at being saved from a certain mauling that he jumped up and flung his arms around the giant, his hands not quite meeting at the back of the man's bulky black bear coat. "Oh, thank you!" Justus gushed, his stiff upper lip melted.

The man patted Justus on the back with a paw. "Think nothing of it," he rumbled. "Men have to look after each other out here in the wilderness—or the animals will win."

Justus pulled back, gripping the man's furry arms. His wide, delighted eyes stared into the other man's calm, brown eyes. "Yes, thank you. You arrived just in time. Who, um, are you, anyway?"

The man chuckled deep in his barrel chest, his thick brown beard rising and falling. "You can just call me … 'Bear.'"

"My guardian bear," Justus exhaled, his pale face, with the beginnings of blond stubble on the cheeks and chin, beaming, his body surging with heat in the grasp of the big man. "I'm Constable Justus of the Royal Canadian Mounted Police," he gasped. He was so overwhelmed by the adventure that he impulsively jumped his head forward and kissed Bear on the lips, getting as much hairy beard as he got red mouth.

Bear dropped his rifle and caught up the little constable in both of his arms, mashed his mouth against Justus's open mouth. The two men kissed passionately, wrapped up together in erotic heat and hunger out there on the bitter trail.

Justus impetuously darted his pink tongue into Bear's maw, his joyous licker bumping up against Bear's heavy tongue, rousing it. The pair excitedly twined their tongues together, the slippery appendages writhing electric like the northern lights overhead at night, their hot, panting breath flooding each other's mouths.

Until Bear broke the exchange by jerking his shaggy head back. "I like your style, Constable Justus," he growled. "But you still have a lot to learn about surviving up here."

Justus licked his trembling lips. "Teach me. I'm eager to learn."

"The way you learn best is by doing."

Bear released Justus, picked up his rifle, and brushed off the snow, then took a giant step back into the bush. "I've got traplines to check on. And you've got a job to do, too."

Constable Justus recovered some of his composure, reminded of his duty. "Yes, yes, I do. Will, um, I see you again?"

Bear lifted his mitt in a gesture of parting, stepping sure-footedly through the underbrush. "I'll be around," he called over a broad shoulder, before fading back into the forest.

Even without an experienced guide to show him the way, Constable Justus continued his pursuit of the man known as Fer Peltier. He still possessed the crude map Thomas Cook had drawn for him on a piece of birch bark, illustrating the way to the fugitive's dugout. And now, thanks to his encounter with the bears and Bear, he also packed in his arsenal a newfound sense of confidence in his ability to operate in the northlands.

He made camp for the night, built a roaring fire out of the branches he hauled out of the bush and beat free of snow. Then he bedded down after a meal of jerky and hardtack. And he was off down the trail at the first pale light of the following freezing cold day, a breakfast of hot tea and biscuits in his belly.

As Justus ably mushed his dogs and handled his sled, he ran a hand over the lower portion of his young face. He grinned, feeling the heavy stubble there, no stopping it. The luxury of civilized shaving was something he had neither the time nor the tools for. Besides, if one was to survive in a new environment—as Justus was determined to do—one had to adapt to it. His cheeks, chin and neck were not so cold anymore. A beard seemed to grow naturally fast on a man near the Arctic Circle.

By mid-afternoon, Justus was thirty miles further down the trail, riding the skids of his sled and occasionally running along behind, wending through the undulating forested landscape. Until the dogs loped over a narrow ribbon of bare snow and the sled and the constable suddenly broke through the crust and collapsed into the hidden stream beneath.

"Darn!" Justus cursed, finding himself sitting in two feet of icy cold water, slush and snow. He hadn't recognized the signs of the covered stream that crossed the trail.

The sled was tipped over into the water, its cargo all wet. Justus pushed up off the smooth pebbles of the creek bed and climbed to his feet. His gauntlets and leggings were soaked, the wool and cotton already stiffening with cold, the sensitive skin underneath already starting to freeze. He knew he had to build a fire, and fast, so he could strip out of his icy duds and dry them and him out. Survival depended on it.

But when he righted the sled, got the dogs to pull it up onto the bank of the creek as he pushed, he discovered that the matches he'd stored in a leather pouch next to his cartridges were wet as well. Useless.

"Double darn!"

The chill was creeping into his legs and blood. His pants and long underwear creaked as he stamped his damp feet and blew into his bare hands. He looked around for two sticks to rub together, took a step forward, and crashed down into the snow. His pants and underwear had already turned solid, heavy, his legs refusing to obey the message his brain was sending them. He futilely beat his hands against the snow.

"Always seal your matches in a waterproof container," a voice said. A deep, thick-chested voice expressed through a heavy beard. And then two strong hands took hold of the fallen Justus and lifted him to his feet, set him tottering upright.

"Bear!" the RCMP officer exulted.

The big man grinned through his beard, pulling off his mitts and pushing back the hood of his bear coat, patting down the uproarious mane of brown hair on his head. Then he cleared a spot on the creek bank and gathered and broke some sticks, piled them up and struck a match he carefully removed from a screw-top tin container. He set fire to the wood, and a blaze soon crackled to life.

"Now, let's get off those wet clothes of yours," Bear said. "Before you die of exposure."

Justus bent at the waist, but his frozen pants and underwear wouldn't allow him to even bend his legs. Bear threw back his bushy head and laughed; he pushed the smaller man over onto his backside in the snow.

Bear yanked Justus's pants off, then the officer's long underwear. And a new kind of exposure was evident—Justus's cock, seemingly frozen rigidly erect.

Bear chuckled softly. As Justus blushed under his blond baby-beard. Then the big man set Justus's stiffened garments down by the fire to thaw and thudded to his knees in between Justus's pale, lean legs in front of the lawman's stuck-out cock. Bear grasped the hardened appendage with a massive bare hand.

"Let's see if we can warm this up, too," he said, looking Justus in the widened eyes. "You wouldn't want to lose *it*."

Justus gasped and shivered as Bear bent his unkempt head down and opened his steaming maw and poured his thick lips over Justus's mushroomed purple cap, then inhaled the entire swollen pink shaft of Justus's cock. He consumed the constable's erection in his hot, moist mouth and throat, sending waves of heated pleasure washing through Justus's no longer chilled body, inflaming his stiff member to throbbing intensity.

"Oh … yes!" Justus groaned, digging his fingers into the snow on either side of him. Watching, and feeling, as Bear bobbed his head up and down, the man sucking tight and wet on Justus's pulsating cock, his sealed lips tugging and soft tongue cushioning.

Justus burned bodily all over, his groin on fire. Bear moved his huge, hairy head faster, sucking cock harder, his bristly beard tickling Justus's balls and inner thighs with additional pleasure.

Until Justus whimpered, cried out, his body jerking upwards off the snow with joy and his cock seizing up and shooting delight inside of Bear's suctioning mouth. He splashed the depths of Bear's throat with sizzling gushes of sperm, flooded the hardy cocksucker's mouth with the basting protein of life. Bear rolled his brown eyes up into Justus's glazed eyes and gulped heartily of the spasming, spurting cock in his mouth, easily swallowing all of the other man's ecstasy.

The trail was cold, as always. But Constable Justus was gamely gaining ground, getting closer to the location of Fer Peltier's dugout. He'd been four days in the wild now, and his thin face had gained a thick matting of blond hair, his blue eyes a gleam of rugged confidence. Justus looked more like a true man of the north now, and he carried himself so.

The dogs and sled and the bearded man at last burst out of the scrub forest and bush and onto the vast expanse of a snow plain, as far as the dazzled eye could see. The hazy yellow sun glittered off the endless blanket of ice crystals, blindingly. Justus blinked his watering eyes, then tried to shield them with a hand. But the glare was too intense.

To add to his misery, a thin wind whipped snow pellets at Justus's face in an endless stream, further blasting his vision. He couldn't look up, couldn't look straight ahead, or to the sides. All he could do was look downwards at the pulled-along sled. And even that didn't help much.

So, that by the time the galloping dogs were only two or three miles across the field of pure-white snow, Justus couldn't see at all. It was too painful to even open his stinging eyes. He was snow-blind. He clung to the sled, not at all sure where he was going.

Directionless, the dogs jogged to a stop, immobilizing the sled and the man in the middle of the snow plain. Justus was lost, with no way of clearly seeing his way to safety. He pounded the handles of the sled in frustration, tears streaming down into his beard from his squeezed-shut eyes.

Then he heard a heavy tramping off to his right. He swung his head around and yanked off his gauntlets and fumbled under his coat for his service revolver, fearful of another animal attack. But he couldn't pry his eyes open. It was just too painful. He jerked his gun out of its holster and pointed it blindly in the direction of the noise.

Something smacked it out of his hand.

"Haven't heard of snow-goggles, I'm guessing," Bear rumbled.

Justus yelped with relief and flung his arms wide open in the direction of the earthy baritone. Bear, on snowshoes, caught the smaller man in his arms and effortlessly lifted him up and set him down in the sled. He briefly fondled the growing beard on Justus's handsome face.

125

"You're becoming a part of this country, all right," Bear said with affection. Then he snapped the dog whip in the air and set the huskies and sled in motion.

When Roderick Justus finally woke up later that night, he found that he was lying on a bough- and moss-stuffed mattress in a rough-hewn dirt dugout, naked, blatantly out of uniform. Bear was bent in between his legs, sucking on his cock.

Justus blinked his eyes, happy to be able to see again, exulted to have Bear blowing him again. He grinned and undulated his engorged cock up into Bear's vacuuming mouth, feeding the bear.

Bear took a long, last pull on Justus's gleaming erection and then popped the slathered stretch of cock out of his mouth and gripped it with a big paw. "Think you can take more of me?" he growled, stroking Justus's wildly beating meat.

"All of you!" Justus breathed, instinctively knowing just what the man meant.

Bear stood up and stripped off his clothes. His huge body was a mass of hard muscle and soft fur. He dropped back to his knees at Justus's cock, let the man pet the brown hair on his chest and belly, tug his own cock into a full and raging erection, fondle his hairy balls to full boil. As he roughly felt up Justus's smooth, pale skin, fingered the man's pink, puffy nipples and rubbed the downy blonde fur on Justus's face and balls.

Then Bear straightened up on his knees and hefted Justus's legs to his chest, clasped them there with one muscled arm. He dug two of the fingers of his other hand into a nearby can of bear grease and lubed his jutting cock, then shot the pair of digits down in between Justus's soft, round, quivering butt cheeks.

Justus moaned and jerked, the man's scrubbing fingers feeling so sensual along his sensitive ass crack, swirling around his dilating pink

126

pucker. And then Justus groaned and jerked, when Bear plugged his glistening, bulbous cap up against Justus's tender asshole.

Bear grunted, and thrust. Justus shivered, and cried out. Bear's hood plowed through Justus's ass ring. Inch after inch of bloated shaft plunged into Justus's anus. Until Bear's heavy balls banged up against Justus's fuzzed buttocks, the big man's enormous, pulsing erection buried inside the hot, gripping sleeve of the smaller man's chute.

"Fuck me, Bear!" Justus yelled, getting a grip on his own rock-hard, numbed cock and stroking, his ass and body bursting with erotic emotion.

Bear grasped Justus's lean thighs tight to his massive, furred chest and pumped his powerful hips. His cock surged back and forth in Justus's anus, stretching, stuffing, stoking, fucking. Justus urgently pulled on his own cock and his nipples, his eyes rolled back in his head. His blasted body rocked to the hammering beat of Bear's reaming cock.

Until Justus was jolted even harder and higher—by ecstasy. Thick, sizzling, white strips of semen jetted out of the tip of his hand-cranked cock and splashed down onto his reddened, bearded face and heaving chest and stomach—Bear-spray—just as Bear brutally split ass and then spasmed himself. The mammoth carnal-vore threw back his head and roared, his churning cock exploding in Justus's convulsing anus. Justus felt his scorched chute burn with Bear's gushes of liquid fire.

Both men heeding the horny, hirsute call of the wild to its jubilant conclusion.

The dugout was Fer Peltier's lair.

"I grew out my hair," Bear/Peltier confessed, hugging Constable Justus tight to his pelted chest, their spent cocks squishing pleasurably together.

127

"You were helping me all along," Justus realized, lovingly stroking the man's beard. "As I was hunting you."

Peltier growled contentedly. "I didn't bludgeon Ernest Rigby. The drunken sharpshooter stumbled in behind the Gold Dust Saloon and knocked himself out on the iron railing back there. But who will believe me?"

Justus softly kissed Peltier on the lips, gently running his fingers up and down one of the man's hairy, humped buttocks. "I do. And so will a court—once Rigby comes out of his coma and tells it. I'll see to that. But you have to come back with me, Bear. It'll look good on you—and me."

Peltier grinned and rubbed his heavy beard against Justus's light beard, in an animal-like display of affection. "All right. I'll *come* with you anywhere you want, constable."

Justus smiled, pressing his swelling cock into Peltier's swelling cock. "How about right here—once again?" he suggested. "For starters."

The pair of hairy lovers grappled and rutted and frotted together, marking their naked bodies as each other's exclusive territories from now on.

T&SA
Natty Soltesz

I hate airports. I know: Everybody hates airports. The hustle, the crunch. Frantic people zipping like pinballs around and into each other. Depressing bars and restaurants that look like hell's way stations.

But the worst, of course, is going through security. The sheer indignity of it all. Take off your shoes, take off your belt. Get computer-eyeball-raped then put *back on* your shoes, your belt. What purpose does it all serve? Couldn't you just choke a bitch with your belt if you were so inclined?

These thoughts went through my head as I approached the security check in the Portland International Airport. Shoes in one hand, bag in the other, laptop under my arm, belt draped across the back of my neck, pants held up by sheer force of will.

Twenty hours ago I'd been in the middle of the ocean, sailing and fishing with my brother. I'd been mapping the course back to shore. I'd been catching, gutting, and preparing our dinner. I'd been a man of decision, a man of action, a man of free will.

That was all gone now. The guy in front of me shuffled forward like a zombie, winced with the pain of having to bin the cell phone he'd been staring into for the last twenty minutes. The two children behind me exuded persistent whines like buzzing refrigerators. All of us had the same placid, resigned look on our face: *Let's just get this over with.*

That's when I spotted him. He was manning the body scanner two lines to the left. A bearded gent, couple years younger than me, devastatingly handsome. His TV-blue TSA uniform shirtsleeves were rolled up to his elbows, revealing his tan-brown, muscled forearms. They flexed as he waved an old lady through the body scanner.

What if I my pants fell down as I was walking out of the body scanner and he instinctively knelt down to pick them up for me but the packed crotch of my underwear bumped in front of his face and I got a boner and he couldn't resist …

"Doesn't need a bin." A gruff voice in front of me. I looked up into the embodiment of bitter disgruntlement: the agent manning the conveyer belt.

"What doesn't?"

He huffed. Grabbed my roller bag by the handle and hauled it out the gray bin I'd just placed it in. Slammed the bag onto the belt and shoved the bin in my face. "Sorry," I said. He shook his head at me, at all of us: the great unwashed.

A chubby black guy waved me through the scanner. I assumed the position: feet on stickers that looked like feet, hands above my head. It swooshed around me like a vortex.

A shrill beep. It seemed to resound through the entire airport. Every eye turned my way. The chubby guy looked at me, looked *into* me, and squared his body for action, for attack.

I guess that's about the moment I remembered the fish-gutting knife I'd left in the lower pocket of my cargo shorts.

The chubby guy took one of my arms. Mr. Beard took the other.

They escorted me through a white door off the terminal, a door you wouldn't even realize was there unless somebody opened it for you. I went through three rooms, deeper and deeper, until I was deposited into an interrogation room. They handcuffed me to my chair, which scared me. Was this standard procedure? Who knew? It's so hard to know when your rights are being violated these days.

I'm not a terrorist. I'm *white*—wait, I know that sounds horrible. But I look like a trust fund kid. Always have. Blond, square-jawed, blue eyed—all 'merican. Aside from the occasional joint and drunk-driving excursion—neither of which I'd ever been caught at—I've never broken the law. But I already felt like a criminal.

"Sit tight," the chubby guy said, twirling the knife he'd confiscated from my pocket between his fingers. "Agent Briggs will be here in just a minute." He smirked to Mr. Beard, who smirked back.

"Who?"

"Don't you worry. Agent Briggs is gonna take *real* good care of you." They shot another look at each other, chuckled. Then just before he shut the door behind him, Mr. Beard shot a glance in my direction. What was on his face? Curiosity? Pity? I couldn't place it.

I sat in that room for over an hour. Surely my plane had already taken off. Had terrorism been in my heart from the start? Sitting there with nothing to do made me *want* to blow the place up, after all. I couldn't hear anything, was the weirdest thing, it seemed completely soundproof, a place out of place, a there that wasn't there. It was uncanny, and my unease grew.

Finally the knob of the door turned, slowly, ominously. The door opened and in came Agent Briggs. He filled the doorway. He was a brute with a Cro-Magnon forehead, a dark scrub of hair. Black stubble covered his granite jaw, like coffee grounds from a particularly bold and acidic roast.

"Well, well. Mr. Audley, is it? Nate Audley."

"I usually go by Nathani—"

"Shut up," he said, and slammed the door shut. His massive hand could've been carved from the same block of wood as the door. "You talk when I tell you to talk. Understood?"

"Yes ..." I started to say it, the natural follow up, but stopped myself. Briggs raised his eyebrows.

"Yes what?"

"Yes ... *sir?*" Briggs looked down at me. He must have been six-feet-five with a body that looked like it'd been constructed from cinderblock—the kind of bricks that give off a radioactive charge. His TSA-issue uniform shirt barely contained his tits, no doubt covered in the same mat of black hair that peeked out from his collar and comingled with the stubble on his neck. His forearms were thick as bowling pins, and the pressed creases in his pants were losing a battle with the circumference of his tree-trunk thighs. Those pants seemed to have been sewn around the bulge in his crotch which—unless he was keeping a grapefruit in there for lunch—was an indication of God's infrequent but potent generosity.

He ran his tongue along the top shelf of his teeth. Frightened as I was, I had a feeling that I wanted that tongue, and that he wanted to give it to me.

"Good boy," he said. He had a cloth bag in his hand and he dropped it onto the table. He leaned his massive ass on the table, crossed his arms in front of his chest. Asked where I was going, where I had been, what I'd had for breakfast three mornings ago, and whether my mother had breast fed me as a baby. Who had I voted for in the 2004 election? Had I ever been arrested? Had I been to Afghanistan? To France? Had I been involved in Occupy? Had I ever passed by one of their camps?

"There wasn't any Occupy in Tulsa," I said.

"Sure there wasn't." Briggs smiled, revealing teeth that were like hunks of ivory some sculptor had hacked into existence after too many glasses of wine.

"We searched your luggage," he continued, lifting the cloth bag off the table. What did I care? Search my luggage, hell, search my apartment back in Tulsa if it's going to get me home sooner ... "We didn't find any other forms of contraband. So, you're lucky on that count." He reached into the bag. "But we did find something ... well, at least, *I* found this interesting." I knew what it was going to be before he pulled it out. On my way out to meet my brother, I'd happened upon an adult bookstore and well, see, I'd been needing a new dildo for a while ...

Briggs revealed it slowly, eight inches of pink silicone, veined and ridged to look like the real thing. I'd found occasion to use it during what was sort of a long, dry week alone with my brother.

He brought it to his face and sniffed it. "Not your girlfriend's, obviously."

"Uh ..."

"Also, nothing hidden inside it. I checked. But we'll still need to know if there's anything inside you. A standard cavity search." He set the dildo on the table, reached up to scratch his jaw. "Something you seem to be fairly familiar with."

He uncuffed me. "Now don't try anything funny. You'll need to strip completely. Nice and slow. Place each piece of clothing on the table as you go." Briggs folded his formidable arms in front of his chest. I took a deep breath. This was really happening. Actually, I didn't know what was happening, but I was somewhere between frightened and turned on and going along with it just the same.

I took off my shirt. I know I've got a great body, smooth and muscled, and it kind of gave me a thrill to be getting naked in front of this guy. I did my pants and socks next, stood there for a moment in my underwear (designer, blue and skimpy). My cock was half hard. Briggs looked me up and down appraisingly.

"Nude, Audley. That means those cute little undies, too." I took a deep breath and lowered my briefs. I could feel Briggs's eyes on me as I placed them on top of my other clothes. I faced him—totally naked and exposed. I tucked my arms across my chest. Briggs looked down at my feet, then all the way up my body to the top of my head. He smirked.

My cock rose, then rose higher. There was not stopping it and soon it was completely hard, pulsating from my pelvis, the bell end peeking out of my foreskin.

Briggs grabbed his crotch—just a quick heft, but things definitely seemed to be growing in there.

"Turn around and place your hands on the table." I did so. "Stay still," he said. I heard him approach me then felt his hot breath on the back of my neck. "I'm going to do a quick pat down, just to make sure you're not hiding any contraband." His placed his rough hands on my soft sides and swiped them up into my armpits, prodding into them and then around to my chest. I got a chill as he ran them back down my sides and across my stomach. He knelt and felt up my ankles then my thighs. He stood and pressed two fingers underneath my balls. With his other hand he felt the smooth mound above my cock.

"You shave it yourself?" he said hotly into my ear. I felt the rough polyester of his uniform against my bare skin, the cold buckle of his belt just above my ass.

"Yes, sir. I've been doing it since high school."

"Very nice, boy," he said, and wrapped his big paw around my cock. He stroked it, sliding the foreskin back and forth over the sensitive head. There was a drop of pre-cum on the tip. He swiped it up with his finger and popped it into his mouth. "Mm," he said.

Moving his grip to the base of my cock, he tightened his fingers around my whole junk, almost enough to where it hurt, to where I knew who was in control.

"Now I'm going to examine your mouth, to be sure you aren't smuggling anything in there. You'd be surprised what some people manage to hide in their mouths." He slid two fingers past my lips and across my tongue. His fingers were calloused and tasted bitter and salty. I tried not to choke as he pushed them down my throat, tightening his grip around my nuts as he did. Slowly he began to remove them. As they passed back over my tongue I closed my lips around them, suckled. "Mm," Briggs said, pressing his crotch to my backside. I could feel his cock, coiled in his pants like a snake ready to strike.

"Now onto the rectal search. Usually we use a glove and some lube but you won't mind if I just do this the old-fashioned way, will you?"

"No, sir."

"I didn't think so." With one hand he spread my ass cheeks until my hole was exposed. "Shave that too, eh?" He took the index finger he'd wet in my mouth and pressed it to my hot hole. I breathed, relaxed, because I knew it was going to be rough. One second his finger was poised there and the next he was shoving his whole fat digit inside me. I gasped.

"Now, now," he said, wrapping his Popeye arm around my bare chest. "This is strictly routine. Just making sure you're not hiding anything up there." He held my body close to his as his finger invaded my asshole, pumping it in and out as he talked. "That's a good boy," he said, turning his finger clockwise and feeling all around my insides. My cock was still hard, and Briggs brought his hand around to stroke it as he fingered me. "Just relax. This is for your own good, your own safety, and the safety of your country."

He pressed down on my prostate, which always drives me crazy. My whole body convulsed and squirmed against his body. He held me tighter and put his lips to my neck. Then he was licking and biting my neck, still working my cock in his paw. "Nice and tight, just how I like my boys," he said. I turned my head to meet his face. Our lips collided and we were making out, his stubbly jaw locked on mine, tongue shoving into my mouth as he fingered me mercilessly.

That was what pushed me over the edge. He kept kissing, fingering, and stroking me as my prostate swelled and my balls contracted up into my body. I was lost, completely out of control, getting reamed and masturbated by this TSA brute. My hole squeezed his finger, the first volley of jizz flying across the desk and landing halfway across. The next shot went all the way across. Briggs never quit, he worked my body until I was milked dry.

Then he pulled out, backed away. He was just a little flustered. I was wrung out.

"Good job, boy. You took it like a true American. I'll tell you what I'm going to do," he said, and began to unbuckle his belt. "To show you my appreciation." He undid his pants, then lowered them and his boxer shorts around his thighs.

There it was. A massive slab of all-American beef, a flesh-and-vein cousin to the Washington Monument. "I'm gonna let you give it a kiss. For your service here today."

I got on my knees and brought my face to his crotch. Briggs's nuts were as big and fleshy as a bull's, his whole crotch a riot of black hair that tangled with the hair on his thighs, his stomach. Tickly little black hairs even traveled halfway up his shaft. He pushed it closer to my face. It smelled musky, animalistic. "Just one kiss, though. Think you can handle that?"

"Yes, sir." I put my lips to the scorching hot shaft. Smooched it, right beneath the head. As I did, pre-cum that had built on his pee hole dripped down his shaft and over my lips. I took my lips away and gratefully licked them clean, savoring the taste of him.

God bless America, I thought.

Briggs, hoisting up his pants, instructed me to "sit tight" while he cleared me "in the system."

"You'll be permitted to leave soon enough," he said, and left. I got dressed. I put the dildo back in the bag in case somebody else came in.

Was Delta going to reimburse me? Probably not. I was most likely out of a six-hundred-dollar airplane ticket and I hardly had enough money to buy another one. I was going to have to call my brother, figure out some way to get back to Oklahoma.

I sat there with my head in my hands, spun by all that had just occurred.

The door opened and in walked Mr. Beard. He glanced behind him as he entered, shut the door quietly, and locked it.

"Hey," he said. "I'm Agent Erdmann." He held out his hand. I took and shook. "Um, so, we're still finishing up the paperwork before we can, you know, let you go."

"OK."

"Yeah, but I wanted to check and make sure you were OK. I mean, Briggs can be kind of rough on guys sometimes."

"It wasn't too bad, I guess."

"Good," Erdmann said. He shuffled on his feet. He was truly adorable, with bright blue eyes set off by his thinning auburn hair. HIs body was thick with a few extra pounds around his waist, but powerful and strong.

"I just thought maybe you could use some comfort after going through an ordeal like that. And well, I guess I should tell you, there's a camera up on that wall." He pointed to a small circle, hidden in the trim around the ceiling. I hadn't noticed it. "So, I kinda watched what happened. And it was really hot."

I felt my cock begin to stir. Just what was going on in this passion pit of an airport? Who cared?

"I'm interested," I said.

"And I think I should tell you, I'm a trans guy." I was surprised,

137

but not uninterested. I nodded. "I know he was pretty rough on your ass, so if you want to take it out on *my* ass, well, I'd be into that, and it might make you feel better." His earnestness was almost hilarious, but who was I to say no to this gorgeous specimen of Portlandia?

"That sounds great," I said. "But I want to make out with you, too."

"Oh, well, OK, sure," he said. I stood and wrapped my hands around his waist, pulling him into me. I kissed him, my face burying in that thick and luxurious beard. His kiss was tentative at first, his tongue kept firmly in his mouth, but the deeper I went the more he opened up to me. I felt all the frustration of my ordeal melting away as this sexy otter gave himself over to me, relaxed into my arms.

My hand naturally went to the crotch of his pants. To feel the soft, rounded presence there thrilled me, but Erdmann pushed my hand away.

"No, no, you don't have to do that …" he said.

"Can I?" I asked. He seemed to think about it for a moment. I tucked the tips of my fingers into the waist of his pants, felt his firm, flat, pelt-covered stomach, teased them further down. Erdmann didn't stop me so I went lower until I felt the folds of his pussy and his engorged clit. "Is this OK?"

"Yesss," he said in a low moan. He was so wet. I'd never experienced anything like this before, but something about that soft, inviting hole on his strapping, hairy body was a total turn on. My cock was ready to burst out of my pants. I undid my pants and let it spring out. Erdmann stroked it a bit, then undid his own pants. He turned around and lowered them over his ass, placing his hands on the table. His ass was a thing of beauty, round and firm as two halves of a rubber ball, smooth as cream and overlaid with fine brown hair.

An ass like that deserved more than just a surreptitious fuck. Whether Erdmann was hoping for a quickie to avoid getting caught by Briggs I didn't know. Nor at that moment did I care. This was all mine, a true gift from the TSA, and I was going to make the most of it.

I got down on my knees. "What are you—?" Erdmann managed to get out before I parted his cheeks and licked up his hairy crack, from the base of his front hole and up past his gorgeous pink asshole. He gasped, seemed to have the wind knocked out of him. "Oh my God," he finally managed to say as I made a feast of his ass, digging my face in there, pressing my tongue deep. I jacked myself as I ate him.

When I stood I was hard and ready. I rode my thick dick against his asshole. That made Erdmann come alive. Clearly he was used to having a cock in that handsome little bum and was ready for more. He squirmed against it, and I almost thought he was going to slide himself on it raw, but even though he kissed the head a few times with his hole, sank it in just a few inches, he finally reached into his pocket and pulled out a condom.

"What about lube?" I asked.

"Oh, yeah," he said, and scooted across the room with his pants still around his ankles. He went out the door and came back a few seconds later with a huge container of Skin Glide. He handed it to me. "We have a whole cabinet. More than three ounces, you know."

"Heh," I said. I was glad at least some of the stuff the TSA confiscates was going to good use. Erdmann resumed the position while I suited up. When I had us both lubed, I leaned forward and whispered into his ear. "You want me to fuck you?" I pressed my cock head to his asshole.

"Yes."

"Say it."

"Please fuck me, sir."

"You like somebody telling you what to do for a change?"

"Yes, sir," he said. "Fuck me, please fuck me." I took it easy on him, slid it inch by inch. Erdmann groaned and cried out like a porno actress. I didn't care if anyone could hear, or see for that matter. All I cared about was that his ass was tight and hot and available to me. I held tight to his hips, pulled back and shoved it in hard. Erdmann squealed. His ass was gorgeous and tan and I was splitting into it, my fat log piercing him right down the middle. I reached in front of him, pressed my fingers into the folds of his front hole, his hot and pulsing little trans-guy cock. That really got him going. He moaned and squirmed back on my cock. It got to where he was giving it to me as much as I was giving it to him. I pulled up his shirt so that I could see the taut muscles on his lower back, like coils of rope buttressing both sides of his spine. This was one seriously hot piece of tail.

"I'm gonna cum soon," I said.

"Oh, do it. Cum in my little ass." I held tight to his hips, held on for dear life as I fucked, my nuts slapping against him with each thrust, my cock going all the way in him from the head to the base and back again.

"Oh, fuck … here it comes … fuck!" I shoved it in him to the hilt, held it deep and creamed away. Shot after shot filled the tip of the condom.

Erdmann seemed pleased with himself when he saw the load I'd blown. "Briggs usually gets all of them," he said, pulling up his pants, buckling them. "He's a bully."

"Sure is," I said. "So, I'm free to go?"

"Oh yeah, sure," he said. "Didn't I tell you that?"

"You said you had paperwork to fill out."

"Did I?"

"Never mind," I said.

"Unfortunately, your flight already left. However, my shift is up and I'm off the next few days. I thought, if you want, maybe we could travel together."

"Oh, really?" I had to admit, the idea of spending more time with this sexy dude was quite appealing. "Do you get free flights or something?"

"Sometimes, but I thought we could take my car."

"Your car …" I said, and broke into a big smile.

He had a convertible. His first name was Evan and he looked completely delectable in his civilian clothes.

We drove for the next two-and-a-half days, taking side roads, blue highways, detours. We fucked our brains out every chance we got and made a mess of two cheap motel room beds. This was the real America, I realized. The America that doesn't suspect the worst, that encompasses all religions, all persuasions. Everyone and everything. The America you don't see when you fly over it.

CHRISCROSS

David Aprys

August in New Orleans was intolerable. Hot didn't begin to describe the weather; humid was an understatement. More like being locked in a steam bath with little hope of escape. Like the sauna in the Richelieu Hotel, where Louis Reynard had helped out during summers in high school. Where his father had been a porter until the day he died.

At dawn the sheets clung to his bare skin. He'd taken a bath before bed, but the night had been sweltering. He could smell himself, ripe and musky sweet, like the bougainvillea draping the latticework on the stairway leading to his quarters over the coach house.

Moaning from horniness and the heat, he ground his erection into the uncomfortable mattress. The window fan didn't help cool things down—and made too much noise. But not enough to mask the banging sound of the screen door.

"Rise and shine," the voice came, low and teasing. "Got something I need you to do."

No use pretending to be asleep. Christopher wouldn't go away until he got what he wanted.

Even at this hour, he whiffed of booze. Probably up half the night playing cards—and losing. Amazing that he'd managed to graduate Tulane, the way he'd carried on. But things came easy to a rich white boy whose father was a federal judge.

"What do you want?" Louis sighed, propping himself up on an elbow. Not that he didn't know.

Chris stripped off his polo shirt and stepped out of his narrow trousers. The early morning light glinted off his mop of dark blond hair. He'd taken to wearing it longer recently, and it mightily aggravated his father. Every day at breakfast the judge told him to cut it— said it made him look like a degenerate from an English band on *The Ed Sullivan Show.*

He came to the bed wearing only briefs and a smirk.

Despite his annoyance, Louis's cock jumped. He'd long since gotten over whatever feelings he'd harbored for Chris, but the kid still had a way about him.

It wasn't just his smooth, tight body, tan from playing lifeguard at Lakewood Country Club, in that summer of 1964. Nor could his boyish face—full-lipped and narrow cheeked—entirely account for the hold he still had on Louis, despite everything.

That hold, Louis thought as Christopher pulled back the sheet, lust clouding his ultramarine eyes, was his depravity.

They'd begun when Chris was seventeen, shortly after Louis, who'd recently had to drop out of Xavier College, started working for Judge Mellon and his wife. Over-friendly to the new chauffeur, Christopher constantly found excuses to visit his room, especially at times he was likely to find Louis half out of his uniform. One night, coming home soused, Louis hadn't exactly been surprised to find Chris naked in his bed.

He'd messed around with other boys at his fancy boarding school in Baton Rouge, Chris explained. And if Louis wouldn't have sex with him, he threatened, he'd tell his father Louis had molested him. Besides, he'd seen the way the chauffeur watched him sunbathing by the pool, while waxing the car in the shade of a venerable magnolia.

And it had been true. Louis's dreams had been haunted by Christopher's lithe body, the provocative way the boy spoke his name, how his round butt filled out his striped bathing trunks. He'd felt guilty imagining whether that ass would be smooth and pale, or covered in soft brown hair, like his bronzed legs. He'd gone crazy, fantasizing about those pillowy lips wrapped around his cock.

Since then, he'd had no need for guilt or fantasy. He hadn't been with another man for months until that first night with Chris, when they'd fucked until the sun was up, in every position and in every corner of Louis's one room apartment. Neither of them could get enough of each other. After that, for too long a time, Christopher was all he could see.

Louis recognized his faults from the beginning—Chris was selfish, cunning, even a little cruel. But he couldn't help himself. Never before had anyone shown him the carnal depths this manchild, seven years his junior, had.

Straddling Louis's hips, Christopher reached for his cock. It leapt under his touch, almost painfully hard. Muttering dirty words, Chris guided it to his pucker. Louis groaned, wishing he'd tasted the lad's pink sweetness first, but when Chris started moving, Louis was lost. His cock sank into the depths of the younger man, his hands gripping hard thighs.

There was no guiding Chris. He'd always known just how to make Louis fuck him the way *he* wanted it. Watching Louis with half-closed eyes, Chris slid up and down on his pole. The breath left his body, and Louis found his eyes straying to the tight muscles of Chris's belly. With each downward stroke, Louis watched Chris's midsection expand. Knowing he was seeing his cock poking the kid's guts made him lose control. He growled like a madman, sweat slicking his bronze skin. How could it feel so good to fuck someone he didn't even like?

Chris twisted his nipples—hard—Louis returned the favor, though by now he could barely focus. He bucked his hips upward. Grabbing Christopher by the hips, he flipped him onto his back. No—this way he still had to see that lying mouth. So he flipped him again, forcing his face into the lumpy mattress, drilling him hard, keeping a vicious rhythm, stabbing that tight ass with his ever-swelling cock.

"You ready?" Louis gasped, on fire. He plunged deeper, his entire body rigid as he thundered out a battle cry.

"Fuck yeah, harder," Chris howled, gravel in his voice.

Then Louis was cumming, cumming and losing his mind, lunging into his enemy, shaking, feverish. He slapped Christopher's ass hard as he could, knew the kid was hitting his own dick with furious strokes, saw him shoot on the dirty sheets, smelled his spunk, didn't care about his pleasure, drove himself deeper, hoping it hurt.

Angry with himself afterwards, Louis trudged to the claw-foot tub in the corner of his room, filled it with tepid water. Chris lit a Pall Mall, tossed Louis the pack. Sliding into the tub, he scowled at the naked blond sitting on the edge of his bed.

"You can go now." He flung the lighter aside and took a drag, glad of the cleansing water.

"Hardly, my dear Reynard," Christopher laughed restlessly. "Fucking's only half of what I want."

"If it's money, I have none left—you cleaned me out, paying your stupid gambling debts."

"A trifling fifteen hundred dollars?" Christopher's voice came out sing-song. "Nothing compared to what I'll come into on my next birthday."

"So, pay me back," Louis huffed, dropping his spent butt into a tin ashtray next to the tub. He looked at Chris, saw that his hand trembled as he ashed his cigarette.

"With mother gone, Grandfather Tourneur's money comes to me," he explained. "You do this one thing, I'll make sure you get paid out."

"What thing are you talking about?"

Christopher paused. Louis thought it was for dramatic effect, then saw the way the younger man's face drained of color.

"I'm being blackmailed ..."

"Let me get this straight," Louis said. Barefoot in the gray pants of his chauffeur's uniform, he rolled up the sleeves of his white shirt. "The blackmailer expects me to come with you tonight?"

Chris rose from the bathtub, drying himself with Louis's damp towel. "Over the phone he said I'm to have you drive me to Audubon Park, but you're to stay in the car. I meet him by the Mumford Oak near the lagoon at midnight."

Louis glanced at the clock. Only half an hour until he had to drive the judge to the courthouse on Royal Street, then wait to take him to lunch at Galatoire's.

"These photographs," he watched Chris carefully. "How bad are they?"

"Worse than bad," Chris admitted, blinking rapidly. It was the first time Louis had seen anything like fear on his face. "I'll be ruined if they send them to Daddy. He might tolerate Negroes, but not inverts. He learns his only son is sleeping with men, some of them colored, he'll make sure I never see a penny of my inheritance."

"Where were these pictures taken?" Louis asked, eyes still trained on Christopher's face.

"That rooming house in the Marigny, where I take my dates." He slithered into his shirt.

Dates, thought Louis with scorn. Christopher didn't even know

146

most of their names, and vice versa. Safer that way, he insisted. Nobody could use his position in society as leverage. Apparently he'd been mistaken. Louis kept quiet, suspicion creeping over him.

Chris exhaled. "There were even a couple photos taken here."

"The hell you say!" Louis shouted. He turned away, not wanting Chris to see his face.

"They must've shot through that window over the kitchen sink." Christopher lit another cigarette. "So you're in this, too. Daddy would throw you out on the street, and you'd never get back that money I borrowed."

"Borrowed?" Louis snapped, trying to keep from shaking with anger. "You stole the last five hundred dollars I had, you spoiled little shit! Now you've gotten me involved in this nightmare?"

"Relax, Louis." His voice shifted to expansive tones. He raised his chin. "I'll put another five hundred on top of what you're owed. Make it a clean two grand." He crossed the room, stroked Louis's arm.

He shook off Christopher's hand. "Suppose they come back—demand more than ten grand?

Chris let out a nervy chuckle and squeezed Louis's crotch. It jumped traitorously in his grasp. "This isn't the first time. They took a thousand off me during Mardi Gras. I was too ashamed to ask for your help, too drunk to figure out a plan. I won't make that mistake again."

He looked Louis dead in the eye, hand still moving over his dick.

"You're my backup, but this time I'm also bringing a gun."

At ten o'clock, apprehension curdling his thoughts, Louis stole another look through the filmy curtains at the kitchen window. He'd done it about fifteen times in the last hour. Lights still shone from the house, but the old judge was a man of regular habits. He'd be in bed soon. Louis poured himself a Scotch, grateful for the numbing effect.

Was there way to dissuade Christopher? Louis was a brave man, had served in the army. There he'd learned the most dangerous man with a gun was a coward—a word which described Chris perfectly.

This could not end well.

Only one light remained on in the main house when he heard footsteps on the stairs.

"We'll take the Corvair," Chris said, entering.

"That piece of crap?" Louis rubbed his sweating palms together.

Chris dropped a small duffel bag by the door. "Less noticeable than the Town Car or the convertible." Sidling up to Louis, he put an arm around him.

"Get off me."

"Nerves got you?" Chris snickered, stepped back to light a cigarette.

"Why aren't you more nervous?" Louis asked, rinsing out his tumbler. "We're both in deep shit because of your recklessness."

"Like you, I've had liquid courage. Besides, I've got my friend along for the ride tonight." He lifted his shirt, showed the Colt pistol tucked between his firm little stomach and the waistband of his pants.

"You're not even a good shot, Chris. Liable to hurt yourself." Louis paced to the coffee table, lit a cigarette of his own.

"Don't be such an old woman," Chris let go another mocking laugh. "The bloodsucking bastard said not to involve the police. As if I would. A boy's gotta have some protection."

"Yeah? Well, I'm waiting in the car." Louis shook his head.

"Lily-livered for a former soldier." Chris crept over to the couch, set the gun on the table, and dropped down next to Louis. "Let's have some fun before we go." He breathed into Louis's ear, unzipping his pants. "Once this is over, you can fuck me all night."

He slid to his knees, eyes glowing. With one hand, he started stroking Louis, with the other, he pulled his own dick through the fly of his khakis. Moaning, he started licking where the conical head met Louis's veined shaft.

Louis leaned back, thinking how great it felt, knowing it couldn't continue. He wanted this thing done. For a minute, he watched the kid's blond head bob up and down, warming to his efforts. He pulled his dick out.

"Once this is over," Louis rose, zipping up, "we're finished, Christopher."

Still on his knees, Chris opened and closed his mouth without speaking. Stuffing his wilting dick back into his pants, he sneered petulantly.

"Suit yourself." He checked his watch. "We need to go soon. Change into your chauffeur's livery. I like my servants in uniform."

Louis shrugged. Wasn't worth arguing with the arrogant little snob.

With a self-satisfied smile, Chris went into the tiny water closet, leaving the door open. Louis stood there, listening to him urinating, eyeing the gun.

They took Magazine Street west—Christopher insisted. St. Charles Avenue would've been faster, but he wanted to be sure nobody followed them. From the glove compartment, he fetched a flask. Glancing back repeatedly, he took pulls from it, not speaking again until they were in sight of Audubon Park.

"Vodka?" he offered Louis the flask.

"No thanks. Someone has to keep his wits."

Christopher lit his umpteenth Pall Mall, started coughing even before he'd taken a decent drag.

"Surgeon general says too many of those things'll kill you." Louis remarked, trying to keep his voice steady.

"Daddy'll kill you if the blackmailer sends him pictures of us butt-fucking." Chris scraped a hand through his hair. "Take the next right, follow the gravel road that goes behind the clubhouse."

"That's a pedestrian path."

"The park's closed, so who's out walking? I want to have the car in case they're armed."

Louis checked the rearview mirror before making the turn. One vehicle behind them, a block away. Just past the golf clubhouse, he took the gravel road. They'd barely gone a hundred yards when the flashing lights came up.

"Fuck—the police!" Chris yelled, shoving the duffel bag under the seat.

"Calm down," Louis said levelly. "And hide that goddamn gun."

Christopher clumsily dropped the Colt on the floor, kicked it beneath him. Cringing, Louis pulled over next to the largest live oak tree he'd ever seen, festooned in Spanish moss.

"Keep your mouth shut unless the cop asks you a question." Louis put the car in park, left the headlights on. His pulse throbbed against his collar. From the corner of his eye, he watched Christopher shift in his seat.

Louis took a deep breath. You could really smell the Mississippi River from here, he thought incongruously. Fuel oil from boats, the briny backwash of the nearby gulf, and a whiff of bourbon, mixed with sweat and desperation. It pervaded this city.

He'd do anything to leave it—and Chris—behind.

The door of the patrol car opened, flashing lights caught the figure of a solitary policeman. Even in the rearview mirror, Louis saw that he was tall and broad-shouldered.

With martial bearing, the policeman approached, flashlight trained on them.

Chris made a pathetic whimpering noise. Glaring, Louis kicked him on the shin, kept his hands on the steering wheel.

"Good evening, gentlemen. License and registration, please." The uniformed cop swept the flashlight over the Corvair's interior.

"Certainly, Officer Russo," Louis read from the cop's shield, then looked into his darkly handsome face. Smiling, he handed over his license. "Registration's in the glove box."

"That's fine, Mr. Reynard." The officer nodded, inspecting the license. Louis reached for the glove compartment. Chris was shaking, sweating, radiating a murky aura of fear. Louis almost felt sorry for the little bastard.

The policeman handed back the license, caught Louis's gaze as he accepted the registration card. Dark eyes and a blunt nose like a prizefighter's in a pleasant, square-jawed face. Silently, something passed between them.

"Step out of the car," said Officer Russo, voice quiet but commanding. "Keep your hands where I can see them."

The blood drained from Louis's face. He opened the car door. If not for his apprehension, he might have laughed at the irony. His parents had warned him: Doesn't matter if you're light-skinned—the police just see a criminal.

"What's the meaning of this, officer?" Christopher demanded.

Louis chortled, couldn't help himself. The kid sounded imperious, like his late mother Lucille.

"I'm arresting this man. The car doesn't belong to him." The cop trained his flashlight on Chris.

"I'm Christopher Mellon, son of Judge Alfred Mellon. The car belongs to me. This man is my driver."

"I don't care if your father's President Johnson. Keep giving me lip, I'll arrest you too." The cop's deep voice sounded amused. Louis couldn't help admiring his brawny shoulders.

Following instructions, Louis leaned spread-eagle against the car while Russo patted him down, first upper body, then his crotch and the length of each leg. The man took his time, and Louis wondered whether this was standard operational procedure.

From the Corvair came a commotion. The passenger door flew open. The policeman stumbled backwards, his flashlight catching Chris's strained face.

In his trembling hands, he held the gun.

"You're not gonna screw this up for me." He cocked the pistol. "My life's on the line. Now yours is, too."

"You don't want to do this." The cop's voice stayed steady. "Step back from the vehicle and drop the gun."

Fear overtook Louis, a white hot flame.

Chris pulled the trigger. Twice. Three times. Nothing happened but hollow sounding clicks.

He threw the gun. It missed Russo by inches, and Chris ran away, toward the lagoon. Weapon drawn, the cop gave chase.

"Don't hurt him—he's just a stupid kid!" Louis shouted, rounding the front of the Corvair.

The cop tackled Chris by the water's edge. In a trice, he had him on his stomach, knee in his back. Louis saw little more than their silhouetted forms, but recognized the sound of handcuffs clicking shut.

He stalked back to the car, pressing the heels of his hands into his eyes. What a fucking disaster.

Even in the light of the waning moon, Louis saw how flushed with exertion both men were when they returned. In one hand, Russo carried Chris's duffel bag.

"Get over here," the cop pointed his gun at Louis. Then he motioned to Chris. "And you, on your knees."

Roughly, he shoved the blond down. As Louis approached, he saw the cop toss his dark hat on the passenger seat along with the duffel.

"Please, let me go—I'm sorry." Chris pleaded, tears streaming down his cheeks.

"Not a chance," the cop replied.

Russo unzipped his black uniform pants and pulled out his cock. It jumped to life, mere inches from Chris's face. "Everyone in town knows you're a cocksucking whore. Why don't you show me how good you are?" With one big hand, he shoved the kid's mouth onto his massive tool.

Still whimpering, Chris slobbered over Russo's meat. Louis felt himself go hard inside his pants watching cop dick stretch that pouty mouth completely out of shape. Hand in his pocket, he started stroking himself.

Russo turned towards him. "Keep those hands where I can see them," he barked.

Louis did what came naturally. Unzipping his pants, he took a few steps closer to where the policeman stood, legs bowed, pumping his cock in and out of Christopher's mouth.

His hair was thick and dark – more than a little wavy. Louis wanted to run his hands through it. Instead, he stood next to the cop, hip to hip. He pulled out his own throbbing dick, letting it stiffen further in the sultry night air, jutting toward Chris.

A thrill of excitement raced up Louis's spine when the officer craned his neck towards him. With an inviting smile, he leaned in. Their lips met. At the same moment, Chris started sucking Louis. Unwilling to break the kiss, Louis lingered, tasting the sweetness of beer in Russo's mouth. He reached down, took the cop in hand, jacking his sticky cock.

Russo groaned, unbuttoning Louis's heavy chauffeur's jacket. It slipped to the ground, hitting Chris in the face as he deep-throated his cock. While Louis stroked Russo's dick, the cop unhooked the closure on Louis's gray wool pants. He stepped out of them, suddenly unencumbered, sweating in the humid night.

Louis helped Russo out of his black uniform shirt and tie. Together, they ripped his damp white T-shirt from his muscular chest. Chris groaned, hungrily lunging at both cocks when the cop stepped free of his pressed pants and white briefs.

The salty breeze played over their skin. Goosebumps rose on Louis's tawny arms as the policeman, naked and perfect, kissed him again, tongue swirling into his mouth. The men pressed their dicks together, offering them both to Christopher.

Louis ran his hands over Russo's pecs and ripped belly—just the right amount of hair, curling and dark, grew at the center of his chest, spread to his nipples. He put both hands behind his head, showing off his bulging arms muscles and furry pits. With his tongue, Louis followed the smooth skin of one bicep to that special musky spot, taking in the cop's masculine scent.

They took turns face-fucking Chris, each of them shoving their cocks into his mouth, choking him. An edgy thrill of power overtook Louis. Chris's hands were still cuffed behind him—nothing he could do to protest harsh treatment. He only liked it rough when he called the shots. But in the headlights, Louis saw the tented front of Chris's khakis, the wet spot made by his straining dick.

"Want out of those cuffs?" Russo asked.

"Mmph," Chris grunted, his mouth full of Louis's dick.

Louis took Christopher's head in his hands, guided his pole all the way in. Behind him, the cop—naked except for boots—freed Chris from the handcuffs, pulled his shirt off. Russo knelt to tweak Chris's nipples, watching Louis slam his cock into the blond's greedy mouth. With his newly free hands, Chris worked Louis's shaft, jacked the cop's heavy prick.

Both men kneeling before him, Louis indulged himself, running his fingers though Russo's hair. The cop's tongue dueled with Chris's on the veiny length of Louis's dick. Both men shared him, brawny cop tonguing the slit of his cock head while Chris slurped his balls. Louis watched them jacking each other, Russo's big one trailing pre-cum, dwarfing Christopher's hand.

Abruptly, the cop jerked Chris to his feet, pushed him against the car. He slapped Chris on the ass so hard it echoed. Parting his cheeks, Russo dropped to one knee. Louis slowly stroked himself, watching as the cop spat in his hand and rammed two fingers into Christopher's hole.

"He's ready for your sweet cock." Russo glanced back at Louis, who grunted his approval, stepping closer.

Chris braced himself against his car as Louis entered him in one thrust. The younger man squealed, edging back against his chauffeur's loins to get every inch inside him. Aching with lust, Louis started jackhammering his ass, sweat dripping down his ribs.

Behind him, Russo parted Louis's ass with strong hands, nestled his dick between the muscular lobes. Frotting wasn't enough for him. Before long, the cop slipped a wet digit into his most secret place. Louis tensed, anticipating.

"Relax baby," the cop cooed, easing in another spit-slicked finger. "New Orleans' finest always pleases."

Louis slowed down, loosened his hold on Christopher's hips. Russo's fingers expertly found his pleasure bud, thumb gently stroking his balls. He bit Louis's neck, rubbing his stubbled jaw against the sensitive skin.

Louis shivered in the heat of the night.

"You want me?" The cop asked, cock pressing, spreading him.

Still deep inside Chris, Louis drew a ragged breath. "Yes, officer," he moaned.

God, how it hurt. Russo's cock was a monster—thick, perfectly shaped for fucking. Louis cried out, feeling every vein, every ridge. Pain ceding to pleasure, his only regret was he hadn't had that thing in his mouth tonight before it went up his ass.

Taking Louis by the shoulders, Russo guided them all. Thrusting into Louis, he drove the other man's dick deeper into Chris. Roaring like a lion, he pistoned, gathering speed. With each stroke, Louis was closer to home, a light growing inside. It intensified, threatened to obliterate. He thrust mercilessly into Chris, driven by the strapping cop fucking the hell out of him.

Sweat-soaked and doubled over the car hood, Christopher growled, made animal noises. Hitting his dick with abandon, he shouted he was close.

Louis pulled out, Russo backed away. Grunting, the cop shoved Christopher to the ground. Kneeling over the kid's face, he jacked Chris's cock furiously. Louis straddled his hips, watched his face screw up. Chris opened his mouth, yelling as his cum spurted all over the three of them.

The light inside him eradicated thought. Louis erupted over Chris's chest. Shaking out the last drops, he rubbed sperm into Christopher's skin with the underside of his too-sensitive dick.

Russo hand still moved in a blur, his cock in the boy's face. The smell of white-hot cum hit the air. Shooting his load into Chris's mouth, he pulled Louis to him with tender force, pawing his sweaty chest, kissing him. Louis forgot everything—his twisted nights with Chris, how much he wanted to leave this town—and found assurance.

Chris pushed up on his elbows, tried but failed to interrupt them. When he tried again, Russo shoved him backwards.

"Asshole!" Chris scuttled from beneath the pair. He picked his way around the car, grabbing shoes, underwear, pants, mumbling to himself. Lastly his hand closed over the handles of his duffel bag.

Standing, Louis found himself rooted to the spot. The cop stood too, wavy hair sticking up in tufts.

"Hey kid come here," he said, positioning his legs wide apart. Chris clutched the bag, approached warily, starting to speak.

156

Before he could say anything, Russo sucker-punched him, a clean uppercut. Chris dropped like a sack of dirt.

"Been dying to teach him a lesson. Not sure how long he'll be out. Let's get lost." He rubbed his fist.

"Did you have to point that gun at me, Nick?" Louis struggled back into his uniform pants. "I took the bullets out of his before we left my place."

"Now he tells me," Nick smiled crookedly, opened the duffel bag to show him the stacks of cash.

"You brought the pictures?" Louis kissed him, anxiety dissolving.

"Yeah, what should we do with them?"

"Throw 'em in the back seat with Little Lord Jackass. By the time he figures out what happened, we'll be halfway to San Francisco …"

SPY GAMES

Franco DiMaso

San Francisco, 1992

Michael's body was gently rocking back and forth as the van moved down the streets of San Francisco. The street lights had already come on even though it wasn't even eight yet. His flight had gotten in late, or he'd be having dinner by now in a nice little restaurant somewhere.

Or getting fucked.

Considering the throbbing bulge in his tight uniform pants, probably the latter. Cabin pressure must have had something to do with it; he couldn't explain it, but every time they landed, he got hard. Which, at times, made him uncomfortable, sitting across from passengers on the cabin crew's jump seats. Folding his hands in his lap as if he were praying usually took care of staying decent. Unless the soft pressure just made him even harder.

He was glad they'd finally arrived—engine troubles had kept the plane on the ground for nearly four hours, and he was beyond exhausted—only his cock was refusing to go down, and he didn't want to exit the crew bus like this.

The vehicle came to a halt, and two porters from the hotel stood in wait, ready to unload the crew's baggage.

Heads turned their way as the twelve of them entered the elegant reception area. It always amazed him the way an airline crew incited such interest. Maybe it had to do with the new, dark blue uniforms that fit snuggly on him and his colleagues, making them look rather distinguished. The pants tailored to a snug fit over his bubble butt; a single breasted jacket over a pressed, long-sleeved white shirt; a matching striped tie; and his polished, black leather shoes.

Yes, the airline's new uniform had gotten him many compliments and, in one instance, even laid. A few weeks ago he'd picked up his first passenger, en route to Los Angeles, and spent the entire night on his back at the guy's house in Malibu, getting plowed in full attire.

Michael got his magnetic key to a room on the twelfth floor and beelined for the elevator. Some of the girls had decided to go out for drinks, but he had passed. No time to waste. He had a date with a hotel full of strangers. Or at least he hoped he did.

With any luck, somebody was ready to play.

In his room, Michael dropped the overnight suitcase and his crew bag in a corner. Then he walked straight to the elegantly decorated room's window without switching on any lights. He scanned the hotel on the other side, looking for windows with lights on and the curtains open. As his eyes slowly wandered over each, most still dark, he scouted for a playdate for the evening.

A few months earlier, on another trip to San Francisco, he had come home one night and looked out the window. He noticed movement in one of the rooms at the Parc Hotel—which was facing his— and, though it was half a block away, he could make out that the people were naked.

And fucking.

159

He had strained his eyes to get a better view, but all he could make out were two naked men against the window, fucking each other standing up. He'd had to use his imagination for lack of close-ups, but he ejaculated on his window after a few moments.

The next day he'd bought a set of binoculars.

He returned briefly to his crew bag and took out the field glasses. The desk by the window came with a lamp and a chair; he positioned the latter right in front of the floor-to-ceiling window. Then he switched on the weak light of the reading lamp on the desk. He was no longer hiding. He wanted to be seen as much as he wanted to watch.

He unbuckled his belt and unzipped his pants but kept his uniform on, then he took a seat and raised the binoculars. He scanned the windows of the hotel across from him again, and this time he could make out two rooms on different floors with people at the windows, their own binoculars raised and scanning Michael's side.

But then he got lucky: a room, well lit, with two people fucking. A woman and a man, both of them very fit from what he could tell. Michael loosened his tie and started unbuttoning his shirt. The smell of the plane and his own sweat were still on him, but he didn't want to leave his spot and take a shower yet. He wanted to watch.

He could clearly see the woman's perky breasts as she lay on the bed, her head arched back. The man on top of her had medium length, dark hair, which fell forward every time he lowered his head. He looked to be well over six feet, his muscular body hard and tight. His round ass slid back and forth as he fucked the woman, and he pulled out every few strokes to expose an enormous cut cock with big, low hanging balls.

Watching porn was fine, but there was nothing better than seeing the real thing, even from a distance.

And then he noticed something. The man seemed to be playing to an audience. He kept pulling his big cock out and slapping it against her skin, all the while looking outside his window at the unseen crowd he performed for. He was getting off on being watched—and who could blame him?

Michael swallowed and licked his lips. He finally caught a glimpse of the man's face, and it was as perfect as the rest of him. The man touched his chest and continued fucking with deep, smooth strokes that came straight from the hip. Then he lowered a hand and put it between his ass cheeks, fingering himself and looking out the window again with a wicked smile.

Michael was so excited he had a hard time holding the binoculars steady, so he put them down for a moment. He sat and pulled down his pants, his hard cock and sweaty balls now fully exposed. He touched them lightly, cupping his nuts and arousing himself further. His pants around his ankles, he leaned back and opened

the lower four buttons of his shirt for better access to his sensitive nipples, which were already getting hard.

He pinched them gently with one hand as he began jerking off with the other, pulling back the loose foreskin and exposing the big, wet head. Then he picked up the field glasses again, switching hands to stroke his dick with his left.

It took a moment, but he found the copulating couple, which had switched positions. The man was now fucking her from behind, and he could make out the muscles in his legs as he knelt there, his pelvis moving back and forth, his butt tight. He pulled out his cock again for everyone to admire. Michael moaned. As tremors rushed through his body, he fantasized about the man's cock driving into *his* ass, stretching *his* hole. Michael was getting close, feeling the blood pump through his throbbing cock. It wouldn't be long now, but he wanted to see the other guy finish first.

And then, almost without warning, the man's body buckled; he pulled out his cock and shot a massive stream of cum on the woman's butt. It happened so suddenly that Michael almost missed it, and he had to stop jerking off for a moment in order to hold the binoculars with both hands.

The man across the street pushed his cock back inside the woman and resumed fucking her, slowly and deliberately. He looked out the window, laughing, riding his high.

"Jesus!" Michael muttered, shooting up. He pressed himself against the cold window, aching to be in the same room with them. He wanted the man to shove his big, wet cock down his throat so he could swallow what was left and lick him clean.

Michael moaned and closed his eyes, then he dropped the binoculars and touched his chest, gently squeezing his nipple. His head smacked forward against the window as a series of intense moans and expletives escaped his lips, ejaculating against the pane, his breathing labored and his entire body shaking from the eagerly awaited orgasm. He gasped for air, and as he opened his eyes he could see his load trickle down the window in long streaks. He rubbed his twitching cock against the glass, trying to prolong the sweet tingle that ran down his shaft.

Jesus, he'd needed that.

He collapsed back in the chair, and after a brief moment he bent over and looked for the binoculars. There were now streaks of semen on his shirt and his cock was still throbbing, dripping onto his abs. He lifted the glasses and looked out. The couple's room was still brightly lit, but the woman wasn't visible anymore.

The guy stood by the window, his cock still impressive but getting soft. He looked over to Michael's hotel, then he closed the curtains.

Show over.

Michael got up and finally undressed in full view of everyone who might be watching, ready to take that hot shower after all.

A glorious morning greeted Michael when he opened the curtains the next morning. Before taking a shower he started up his Toshiba laptop. He felt frisky and wanted to try another one of those chat sites he'd recently discovered, see if anyone was up for meeting in real time.

He switched on the light in the bathroom and looked at himself in the mirror. At five-foot-ten and one hundred and forty pounds he wasn't a massive guy. In fact, he felt downright skinny next to most guys at the gym, though his lean and defined body certainly had its admirers. Since turning thirty, three years ago, he'd been working out more in the hopes of putting on some muscle.

Michael wasn't beautiful but he'd been quite popular lately. He was the kind of guy people needed a second look to notice—unless they saw him naked and got a glance at his big, uncut cock or bubble butt. His face was angular, with piercing, watchful dark blue eyes that often appeared black. He had a winning smile that people always complimented him on, and he wore his dark, blond hair short. Today, he looked pretty good. Well rested, a nice tan from a trip down south a few weeks ago, and his chest had grown an inch over the past few weeks. Maybe the hours at the gym were finally paying off.

He brushed his teeth and took a shower, shaving his balls while he was in there. He was ready for whatever might come his way.

But twenty minutes later the modem refused to connect to the Internet. It beeped and burped and hissed for ages, but the connection kept failing, and he got frustrated fast. This Internet thing was certainly interesting, but it seemed they hadn't really figured it out yet. He wasn't patient by virtue, and waiting for hours to get online in the hopes of *maybe* finding someone to fuck was too much of a hassle.

He got dressed and decided to have breakfast. He checked his watch. He'd have all day to himself, but he wanted to be back by five. A quick nap before the crew call at eight, and then they'd be headed back to JFK.

He left the hotel with a small backpack, walked down to Union Square, and caught a bus over to Castro. He got off one stop earlier so he could swing by Tower Records. He picked up two new albums by artists he liked, and on his way to the cashier he noticed that personal CD players were on sale. He decided to splurge and got one.

He paid and walked over to a small restaurant on the corner of Market and Castro. He sat outside and enjoyed watching the people as they walked by. He should have brought his camera. He'd started shooting guys naked three years ago; his collection was growing, even though he was often too shy to talk to people on the streets. That was one of the advantages of the chat rooms: a lot less inhibitions.

After breakfast he walked around the Castro for a while until he ended up in Dolores Park. He sat there, enjoying the day and his new music, even though he noticed that his new CD player regularly skipped when he moved too quickly. This thing was supposed to replace the Walkman, but apparently they hadn't yet completely figured it out.

Around three, he headed back towards the hotel to grab a bite. Someone in the crew had told him about an Italian place around the corner, but when he got there it looked closed. Then he spotted a lone couple in the far corner. Well, at least there wouldn't be a wait.

"May I help you?"

Michael hadn't heard the guy approach him from behind and he was startled. "Table for one, please," he said.

The guy was almost his height, with short, dark hair and matching eyes on a beautiful olive skinned face with a few freckles around the nose. His eyes lit up as he looked Michael over and he exposed perfect teeth. He wasn't Italian, but he had a distinctive European look.

"Certainly. Follow me?" the guy replied with a wink. As Michael followed, he checked out his backside. He wore a white dress shirt and black pants that fit snuggly over a perfectly shaped ass.

At the small table, Michael set down his backpack and took off his jacket. When he ordered a coke with no ice, the guy nodded and flashed such a beautiful smile that Michael blushed from the attention.

The guy's name was Arturo, which didn't sound European. Michael always believed that flying the friendly skies and traveling the world had given him a better insight into people's ethnicity. But maybe he was just fooling himself.

"Let me know if you need *anything else*," Arturo said with a smile before walking away. As he left, Michael checked out his ass again. Heaven.

He ordered some pasta when Arturo returned, and took out a book he bought before leaving Manhattan. But he didn't get the chance to read.

"So, where are you from?"

Michael shut his book and looked up, smiling. "Manhattan."

"Cool. We stopped over there on my last trip overseas. My mom's family is from Greece. My dad is Mexican," Arturo explained.

So, he'd been half right, Michael thought, discreetly checking the man out as they talked. Arturo's shirt hinted at a nice chest, and his pants fit as snuggly in the front as they did in the back, presenting a nice-sized package.

"Are you here on vacation?" Arturo asked. With just one other table to wait on, he obviously had little to do.

"No, work. I'm on a layover. Airlines."

"Wow, that's great. I'm sure you get to see the most exciting places," Arturo enthusiastically replied, scoring major points without even knowing it. The usual response was, "Wow, that's great. I'm sure you get to fuck guys all over the place." There was a reason his friends referred to flight attendants as "air mattresses," but Michael was too shy and unadventurous to claim that title. Contrary to popular beliefs, not all of them had a different lover at every port. "I wish I could travel more. Maybe I should come back to New York …"

Michael blushed. "Yes, you should …"

When Michael's food came, Arturo gave him some space, but continued to watch him from afar and smiled whenever Michael gazed in his direction. *What an incredibly sexy guy,* Michael thought as he ate.

"So, when are you heading back?" Arturo asked upon returning to clear the table fifteen minutes later.

"Tonight." Michael made a face.

"Wow, that's a shame. What time?"

Michael liked where this was headed. "Pick up's at nine."

"I get off at seven." Arturo smiled.

Michael opened his mouth to speak but then quickly closed it. His cock was filling with blood and his heart was racing. *What the hell was he waiting for?* "I'm over at the Nikko, room 1213," he finally managed.

"Can't wait," Arturo replied with a wink and a smile before walking away.

Michael walked back to the hotel, a raging erection pushing against his underwear. He was tempted to jerk off the minute he got back to the room. He couldn't wait to feel Arturo against his skin, to undress and discover his body inch by inch. It was now past five and he decided to pack his bags, prepare as far ahead as he could, and then take a nap.

He didn't think sleep would come as he couldn't stop fantasizing about the things he would do with Arturo, but eventually he drifted off.

When he woke it was almost eight.

Shit, what had happened? Arturo was supposed to be here already, covered in cum. In ten minutes, Michael would receive the hotel's prearranged wake up call, and then he'd have just an hour to get ready.

He was immediately disappointed. So much for all the flirting. Why act all interested if you weren't going to show? Some people were players, but Michael hadn't gotten that vibe from the waiter.

He got out of bed and headed for the bathroom, where he brushed his teeth and shaved. The reception called just before he hit the shower to let him know pick-up would be in sixty minutes. He emerged refreshed and clean a few moments later, then he dried his hair and started to get dressed. The sun had set and he could make out the lights of the hotel across the street. Maybe he'd have time for another peek before he left. He packed away his laptop and finally put on the pants of his uniform, along with a fresh white shirt. He looked at himself in the mirror as he tied the knot of his tie, then stepped into the freshly polished black shoes and put on his belt.

Just then he heard a knock at the door. Probably one of the girls in his crew on her way down. But when he opened the door, he found Arturo standing there, an apologetic look on his face.

"I am so sorry," he said. "Am I too late?"

"What happened?" Michael asked, pleasantly surprised to see the sexy man.

"The waiter from the second shift was late."

"That's alright, come on in," Michael said, happy to be able to see Arturo for a few minutes.

"Are you on your way out?" Michael checked his watch and told him thirty minutes. Arturo's face lit up and a mischievous smile crossed his face. He looked Michael over and nodded. "I love your uniform. Very becoming."

Michael laughed. "Thank you."

"Put on your jacket."

"What? Why?"

"Just do it," Arturo said gently. Michael complied. Arturo looked him over and smiled, then he took Michael's hand and led him to the window. "Do you have any idea how hot you look in this?" he asked, his back pressed against the glass. He caressed the fabric of Michael's uniform. "This has always been a fantasy of mine."

Michael laughed. Arturo gently took his face in his hands and pulled him in, their lips touching. Arturo faintly tasted of gum and his full lips were incredibly soft. After a few shy kisses, their mouths opened and they began exploring each other's tongues. Soft moans escaped their mouths.

Arturo unzipped Michael's fly and he put his hand inside, gently looking for the hard-on he knew was there. He freed the cock from the confinements of Michael's underwear and began gently stroking the warm shaft.

Michael moaned. "We don't have much time," he said.

"Then let's make every minute count."

Michael took a small step back as Arturo unbuttoned his own pants. A big, uncut cock flopped out, smacking against Michael's hard-on.

"Jesus!" Michael exclaimed. But before he could get on his knees to attempt to deep-throat the monster, Arturo shook his head and said, "No, let me."

He pushed Michael back another step, then bent down and took his cock in his mouth. Arturo reached behind him with his hands, spreading his exposed cheeks and pressing his asshole against the cool window pane. Michael groaned and looked at their reflection in the window. Arturo cupped Michael's balls with his hand and swallowed his cock all the way, over and over. When he took a break and stood up, Michael kissed him deeply for a moment, then turned him around as he got on his knees. He'd thought about that ass ever since meeting Arturo, and he dove for it without a second thought.

The sexy waiter must have taken time to shower, because his hole was fresh. His butt was completely hairless and Michael was in heaven. When Arturo arched his back and relaxed, his asshole opened up like a flower. Michael had never seen anything like this, but it drove him wild. He inserted his tongue as deep as he could manage, then he reached between Arturo's legs and gently stroked the fat, uncut cock he was already lusting for. Arturo's moans were low and long, and his body trembled with excitement, pushing his eager hole into Michael's face.

Michael could have eaten his ass all night, but the clock was ticking and Arturo knew it. He turned around, facing Michael again, and got back down on his knees, his back to the window.

"Let me do this for you," he said with a wink. Then he swallowed Michael's cock whole in one slow gulp. He was clearly a pro; Michael's eyes rolled back in his head, savoring every second. His breathing became more labored the longer he fucked the back of Arturo's throat.

He stood there in his suit and tie, putting both hands against the window as Arturo worked his magic. Had he not opened his eyes at that moment he wouldn't have noticed the faint, red light dancing over their bodies. It took him a moment to realize what it was: the light from a camera with infrared sensors.

Someone at the hotel on the other side was taking pictures. For a second Michael wished his binoculars were handy so he could see who it was. He was even harder now, loving the fact that someone was getting off to him getting a blow job, and his nipples perked up as he felt a warm sensation build. He moved his pelvis gently to meet Arturo's mouth halfway.

"Jesus, I'm gonna cum ..." he moaned, trying to take a step back and pull out. But Arturo grabbed his butt and forced the cock back down his throat. It felt as if he'd inserted it directly into his food pipe, and he didn't gag or choke as Michael forcefully ejaculated into it seconds later.

"Oh fuck, yes!" Michael's body convulsed and shook as he cried out and gasped for air, emptying his balls into Arturo's eager mouth. The young man never stopped sucking him, and when Michael quieted down and his body's tremors slowly ebbed away, he kept licking him until his cock was completely clean.

"Oh my God, that was fucking amazing!" Michael panted. Arturo smiled up at him. A huge load of cum was plastered all over Michael's polished, black shoes, and it was only then that he realized his new friend had also cum, without making a sound.

"Someone's taking pictures of us," Michael laughed, catching his breath.

Arturo looked up and smiled. "Good."

He got up, making sure his cum-covered cock wasn't brushing against Michael's clean uniform, then he reached down and gently put Michael's still semi-hard member back into his pants, careful not to hurt him as he zipped him up.

"Thank you—that was fucking great," Arturo said, kissing Michael tenderly and making him sample his own cum. "And very tasty …"

Michael laughed, realizing he'd just served his first meal of the day.

And his shift hadn't even started yet.

WHAT THE DOCTOR ORDERED

Joe Thompson

"You have to fuck me," I said in a breathless whisper as I pulled my lips away from Dr. Demassio's. I was naked, rock hard, and without waiting for a reply, I hopped up onto the padded examination table behind me.

Dr. Demassio was exactly what I loved in a man: older—probably late thirties or early forties—dark haired, and fit. He also looked like a doctor: black dress shoes, black socks, fitted gray slacks that gathered at his crotch, white shirt and tie, and a long white coat with a stethoscope around his neck.

I'd come into UCLA's Student Health Services to get my final hepatitis vaccination. I'd never seen Dr. Demassio before, but upon his entering the sterile exam room I knew right away that he was gay, and that made me feel safer, more willing to speak honestly about personal topics. Plus, he was hot.

During the appointment Dr. Demassio had quizzed me on safe sex practices, and through the course of our conversation I admitted to never having had a real medical physical. He suggested I get one.

"Want me to drop my pants?" I asked with a grin.

Dr. Demassio looked at me, obviously startled by my forward question. However, in the four years I'd lived in Los Angeles, I'd learned that being aggressive could help now and then. Besides, I suspected there was some heat there. Now it was time to confirm it.

"I have time," he said, smiling. I got undressed.

As the physical exam began—with his latex glove-covered hand taking my nuts and gently squeezing, feeling for any foreign bumps—I asked if he was single. (He was.) His warm fingers then pressed into the soft space between my nuts and thighs, feeling for a hernia. He told me to turn my head and cough. I did, then felt the tingle in my dick.

"You going to check this?" I asked, moving his hand onto my hardening shaft.

He pulled away, and for a second I thought I'd fucked up. Bad. I felt panic, like he was going to call my mom or something—which was ridiculous because I was a senior in college. But then I saw him relax, the nervousness leaving his eyes as his gloved hand returned to me, gently wrapping around my dick. I couldn't hold back, so I took the edges of his white coat and pulled him into that deep, intense kiss.

I'd had a doctor-patient fantasy for a long time, and since Dr. Demassio was clearly a "hotportunity," I decided to take advantage of the situation.

It was then I demanded that he fuck me.

He smiled, leaned in, and kissed me again. It was strong, in control, and I instinctively wrapped my bare legs around his waist. "Not here," he whispered, pulling his mouth away. He then broke free of my legs, picked up my shirt, and tossed it back to me. "I get off in thirty minutes." I stared at the bulge in his gray slacks, neatly framed on each side of the white coat. "There's nothing sexy about this place. Believe me."

I didn't. I'd watched plenty of porn scenes with doctors and patients. I knew how a doctor could order the patient into various positions, examine his cock and balls, probe his mouth and butt. I'd beaten off plenty of times to this scenario. Dr. Demassio was sexy, this moment was sexy, and I was sure that if given the chance I could make this an amazing moment for the both of us.

But the doctor was in charge, and it was clear I wasn't going to get any action here.

An hour later, and we were driving in the doctor's convertible BMW up to a swank Mid-Century home above Sunset Plaza. It was dusk, the sky was turning pink-orange, and the warm summer air brushed across my face as we drove up those winding streets. I smiled, thinking about how romantic it all seemed.

Dr. Demassio's home was modest compared to others on his street, with a sweeping white interior and tan leather furniture. But the views from his floor-to-ceiling windows spanned Beverly Hills, West Hollywood, and all the way to downtown.

He was as I imagined a gay doctor to be: wealthy, successful, and confident in his own skin.

"So, what did you want me to check in the exam room?" Dr. Demassio asked with a smile. He leaned in, his big arms holding me tightly against his body. I could feel his dick pushing through his slacks and against my stomach, growing harder by the second.

"I don't suppose you have one of those lab coats lying around …?" I asked, wondering what probing devices he may have in the bedroom.

He laughed. "I know, right? Some guys are really into the doctor-patient thing …" A hint of judgment lay behind the laugh—clearly he didn't share this fantasy—and I felt a bit let down as he slowly lowered me onto his tan leather couch.

Regardless, while Dr. Demassio's hands undressed me, I imagined myself back in the exam room atop the tan, padded examination table. His soft fingertips slid lightly next to the elastic crotch of my briefs as he pulled my pants off. I sat up slightly, letting him lift my polo shirt over my head. The back of his hairy hand brushed my small, tight nipple and I gasped; Dr. Demassio's hands sparked a tingling rush in my body, causing my hard cock to instinctively press against my 2(x)ists.

"I'm leaking," I whispered, seeing the pre-cum staining the briefs at the tip of my dick. I pulled them down and off my legs so he could see the pooling droplet on my dick head. I wanted him to lick it, to taste my sweet seed, but instead he ran his thumb over the drop and wiped it clean. He then took hold of my dick and started slowly stroking.

"What do you like to do?" he asked. I immediately squirmed. I was here, naked, ready to do whatever he suggested. Why, I wondered, was there a need to ask?

"Suck my dick," I said, for lack of anything better to suggest. He nodded, wiped the tip of my dick again to make sure it was clean, and started to suck.

He was good. His lips were warm, his tongue was wet, and he moved at a good pace, keeping his hand gliding up and down my shaft as he moved his mouth over me. But it was only *OK*.

I looked at the tan leather couch, once more thinking about the examination table. I opened my legs—one going up the back of the couch, the other off the front—giving him total access to my body. As he moved himself in between my open legs, I pictured the white doctor coat still on his back, enveloping both our bodies like a cape. My feet would press up into the stirrups of that table in the patient room, and Dr. Demassio would tell me to stop squirming. And when I refused he would take his belt off and strap my right wrist to the metal rod on the side of the table. From there he would remove his tie, using it to restrain my other arm on the opposite side.

I squirmed on the couch, loving the way my sweating body made my back and butt slick. I moved my hips in a circular motion underneath his mouth, letting him know I liked this. He removed himself.

"Squirrely, are you?"

"You're hot," I said simply, keeping my arms and legs submissively locked in place on the couch. Dr. Demassio smiled and went back to my shaft, licking me down to the balls. I started to lift my hips, to give him access to my ass, but the doctor just took hold of my dick and sucked his simple suck once more. I settled back onto the moist leather.

My mind wandered again, back to the exam room, back to my bound wrists and splayed legs. I thought of him putting on latex gloves and stroking me with their sterile, rubbery surface. I would adjust my breathing, trying to control myself, but he'd know what I was doing. He was a doctor. They know how the body works, how the mind works to control the body, and they have the knowledge to outsmart you. So with one hand on my cock, and his eyes locked on mine, he would take his second hand and gently probe a finger into my hole. He would turn it, finding my soft spot, and push into me, sending a small sample of seed out of my piss slit.

"You like that, don't you?" he would ask.

"Yes," I said out loud.

"You can't control yourself," he would inform me, inserting a second finger into my tight bottom. "You know that, right?"

"Yes," I said aloud again as my imaginary scene synched up with the reality of Dr. Demassio sucking my dick.

"You will cum when I want you to cum …" I heard him say—and without warning, I did.

My back flexed tight on the slick, sweat-covered couch, and my hips pushed up into the real doctor's face. I let my cum fly and he quickly pulled his face off. Thick creamy hotness flew from my body, hitting his dress shirt and tie. I looked up and saw cum on his lips, having unloaded some into his mouth.

He turned his head to the side in disgust, looking for a place to spit, until he finally lifted his sleeve and deposited my mouthful onto it.

"Warn me!" he said, clearly pissed. He used his other sleeve to wipe his face clean. He then got up and went straight for the bathroom, leaving me naked, damp, and dripping on his couch. I'd cum, but I was unsatisfied, horny for a real fantasy to be discovered.

"You came in his mouth?" laughed Donald, putting his martini down on the bar so that he wouldn't spill any precious liquid in the process. At 70, Donald was my gay mentor. He'd seemingly lived it all, owning one incredible story after another about his and his friends' escapades—and the lessons learned from those escapades—over the years.

We'd met at a Silver Lake piano bar. I was there waiting for my perpetually late friends to arrive. Donald and I got to talking. Two years later, we were still friends and meeting whenever I needed to discuss my dirty relationship woes.

And when I needed a sexy uniform to wear on a hot night out.

It was fourth of July weekend and the local leather club was having a uniform party. I knew Donald could hook me up with something to wear, and he did: his old Marine Dress Blues.

The look was one hundred percent official. White service hat and gloves, midnight blue dress coat with gold buttons, the regulation white belt, midnight blue pants with the ride stripe running down the side, and Donald's impossibly shiny black dress shoes. He'd even left on his rank and pinned a couple medals on for good measure. The only thing non-regulation about the uniform were my white undershirt and gold toe dress socks—no briefs or boxers, but I did wear my silver cock ring just in case I got lucky.

I felt incredibly tall dressed like this, much bigger than my five-foot-seven frame. And it seemed like others could sense that as well, turning and nodding to me with respect when I entered the bar. Initially I'd been nervous about wearing the entire outfit and possibly staining the white gloves or hat, but this feeling bypassed those concerns. Besides, Donald wasn't worried, saying he was hopeful I'd get some action from wearing them—something he rarely enjoyed during the pre-Don't Ask, Don't Tell days when he served.

Yes, Donald probably got off on my stories and seeing me dressed up. Who cares? He never made a play at me, nor did he ever judge, and I loved him for all those things.

"I got caught up in the fantasy," I said, laughing with him.

"But not in the guy," Donald said. I shook my head. "You just wanted him because he was a doctor?"

"Pretty much," I said.

Just then, a tall, brown-haired guy walking to the outdoor patio got jostled by the nearby dancing crowd. He slipped, and his muscular frame fell into me. I leaned into the bar, accidentally knocking over Donald's martini. The cool wet liquid splashed down onto the blue dress pants and black shoes.

"Shit! I'm so sorry," the fresh-faced guy responded. Though he was clearly older than me, he seemed a lot younger. He wore jeans and a T-shirt, and had wavy hair that looked like it never stayed in place after a combing. On the surface there was nothing special about him, but his face lit up when he looked at me, and I felt a tingling excitement at the base of my chest.

"Someone's gonna have to dry clean those pants and spit shine those shoes before they give them back," Donald said, grabbing cocktail napkins to wipe up the bar.

"Sorry, let me buy you guys a round."

"Kettle one martini, with a twist," Donald spat out quickly. "What's your name, handsome?"

"Sam." He shook our hands, but his eyes lingered on mine a second longer as I introduced myself. He was probably twenty-eight, really fit, and from what I could tell he was too clean cut for tattoos or piercings. I was pretty sure he didn't even have body hair.

And yet that excitement continued to well up inside me.

"You here with friends?" I asked.

"He is now," Donald said, pushing me aside. "Belly up to the bar, handsome Sam, and tell us everything about you."

Sam laughed, smiling big and revealing a small gab between his two front teeth. It was dorky, nerdy, cute. And for some strange reason, I wanted him.

"What do you like to do?" Sam asked at his apartment—and in that instant I was turned off. Bored. I hated guys who asked that. I wanted them to just read the situation, figure it out, instinctively try things, and know when something worked. Guys who couldn't do that—like Dr. Demassio—who asked that question always ended up being a disappointment.

"Do you like to kiss?" he asked, trying to get something out of my silence. He smiled, his hands holding the hips of my blue pants as he swayed his body back and forth with excitement. "Want me to give you a message?" I looked around his apartment—plain, with hand-me-down furniture like my own. I suppressed a yawn. "Let me grab something from my room," he said, disappearing.

My mind shot back to Dr. Demassio's office and what didn't happen there. I glimpsed at the fantasy gone sour, the salvation I'd found in my own dirty mind, and suddenly my blood boiled. Tonight needed to be different. I was horny. Not just for a cum shot, but for something new, something that would set my mind and balls on fire. And if Sam wasn't going to provide it, I'd make it happen myself.

As he returned with a toiletry bag, he started again. "Maybe we should—"

"You dirtied my shoes," I interrupted. For an instant I wondered where the voice had come from, deeper than what I normally sounded like, but it felt so organic, so right, that I followed it by snatching the bag from Sam's hands. I tossed it on the couch and pressed him down to his knees.

Sam's eyes flickered with excitement, then turned small and sheepish. He bent his head down and looked at my once-shiny shoes. He then took off his T-shirt, knelt in a lunge, gently lifted my right blue pant leg, and placed my shoe on his knee to clean it.

"Do it right," I said, moving my right foot and pushing it into his crotch. Even through the sole I could feel his hard shaft in his pants.

Sam's eyes were on fire but his face remained obedient as he placed my foot back on his knee once more. He took his tongue out, quickly licked the top toe area, then spat on the foot and wiped it.

"Good boy," I said, tousling his wavy brown hair with my white gloved hand. Sam smiled slightly from the compliment. He continued on, making his way around my right foot, then gently removing my shoe and placing it on the couch. He paused at the sight of my gold-tipped socks, sniffed then hungrily, then repeated with my left foot. No words were spoken; I couldn't believe how hard I was just from watching someone clean my shoes.

Once the second shoe was off, Sam reached up and unzipped my pants, leaving the top button secured. My tool rolled out, silver cock ring pressing it forward, and I watched as he studied my cut shaft.

"Service me," I said simply. Sam opened his mouth gently, and I shoved my dick inside, watching his entire body relax. He inhaled me into his mouth, and I felt a wave of joy rush over my back, across my chest, through my hips, and into my dick.

"Yes, boy," I sighed, letting my head relax back as my gloved hand held his head in place. Sam was a boy, eager to please me, to make sure he was doing exactly as he was told, making sure I was pleased with his behavior.

I loved it.

"Relax your mouth," I said. "Take me in."

He did, and my dick smoothly slid down his throat. His nose hit the cock ring and his chin rested on my balls. He gagged, but didn't pull off at first, holding on as long as he could. When he did remove his mouth, strings of spit hung from my wet dick and his wet lips.

Sam looked at how my dick poked out of those blue pants, at the silvery saliva on my rod, and once again his eyes grew alive. He dove right back onto my dick, taking it in deep once more. Small tears leaked from the corners of his eyes as he deep-throated me, but he refused to give up, showing me just how strong he was.

I gently reached down and wiped them away. He was a good kid, and I needed to give something back.

Sliding my hands under his pits I pulled him to his feet. He stood rigid while I examined his body. As I suspected, he only had a sprinkling of hair between his beautiful, sculpted pecs. I looked at his face—so smooth and innocent, with a nervous grin over not knowing what was to come. After a second I nodded, and he carefully unclasped my white belt and lowered it onto the couch next to my newly shined shoes. He then undid my dress coat, one gold button at a time, until he could slip it off my body to reveal my white undershirt. I stood watching as he gently folded the coat onto the couch, showing great care with each movement.

Pleased, I lowered myself down and opened his jeans. He wore white briefs, and as I pulled them and his pants off his body I ran my nose along his shaft, teasing him, smelling him.

"Who's cock is this?" I asked.

"What?"

180

"Who's cock is this?" I didn't yell it or growl it or make it too forced. It was a simple question—like a teacher to a student—and I wanted to hear his answer.

"It's *your* cock, sir," Sam responded politely. I nodded, put my hands on his hips, and turned him away from me. My gloved hand then pressed into his lower back and he bent over. He had a small butt, but perky, and perfectly round for his height. I spread his ass cheeks and licked his puckering hole. My tongue slowly slid into it, and I felt him tense up—but just as quickly he relaxed again. He tasted salty, and smelled of man sweat.

"And who's hole is this?"

"It's *your* hole, sir."

I turned him around again and guided him onto the couch. As he watched, I stroked him, the thin, soft white fabric preventing our skin from touching. My hand moved slowly, up and down his long shaft. It felt different, but not just because of the physical contact. There was something else, something inside me that was churning, but rather than think on it too hard I slowly ran my tongue along Sam's taint, over his balls, and then took his long cock into my mouth. The tip was slick and salty from his pre-cum, which made me want to swallow even more of his sweet boy meat.

"Oh God," he whimpered, and his body shook. He was getting close, and we'd only just started. I took my mouth off him.

"You don't cum until I tell you to cum," I said. "Understand?" He nodded. I went back to sucking his dick, but Sam's hands gently pushed my head back. I looked at him, saying, "I'm going to suck you right now. And you are not going to cum. Do. You. Understand. Me?"

"Yes, sir," he nervously whispered, and with a nod I licked his balls, then put his cock in my mouth. As I sucked upward, I pulled off, then ran my tongue down to where the shaft met his body. Again, my mouth went on Sam's dick and he whimpered some more, so I removed it and went back to his hole. I continued, over and over, sucking until he shook or shivered, goose bumps on flesh, then taking my warm, wet mouth away from his unbelievably hard cock, never letting him go over the edge.

"You have to fuck me," he whispered, just as I had to Dr. Demassio.

Suddenly, in that instant, everything made sense: The throbbing urge I'd needed to satiate was power. I'd wanted Dr. Demassio to have it over me and my body, just as I had the power over Sam right this moment. And the uniform, whether it be a doctor's coat or my Marine Dress Blues, conveyed that intensity, giving one person control—of the scene, the emotional story, and the other man.

That was what I'd wanted. It was what I had right now. And I was going to enjoy every second of it.

Sam pulled at my white undershirt, and with uncanny confidence I pushed his hands away. The gloves were wet from my spit and Sam's sweat, but I didn't care. "I don't get naked for you," I said. "Not until you've earned it." I opened the toiletry bag and found the lube, squirting it over his ass and hole. "Finger yourself," I said. Sam complied, slicking the liquid up into his hole, getting it ready for me. I watched as I found a rubber, opened it, and rolled it on my tool. For a moment I stared at my hard cock and big balls, the silver cock ring pushing them out from the fly of my blue marine dress pants. I looked fucking hot.

"Lube my cock," I said, and Sam obliged, stroking my shaft with the slick liquid while still fingering his own hole.

"You ready?" he nodded, removing his two fingers. I pulled his legs toward my hips and pressed my dick head against him. Sam's hands gripped the couch, ready but nervous. I slapped his puckered hole with my cock and it relaxed, so I slowly eased the head in.

Sam gasped and I stopped. "Please …"

I shushed him, gently rubbing my hand on his cheek. "It's OK," I whispered softly, leaning in to give him a light, sweet kiss. "You're my stud. You can do this." Sam looked me in the eyes. "Yeah, keep staring at me. I've got you …" He loosened up and my dick slid right in. His hole was dark, warm, and strong, clenching onto my cock and holding it inside.

Sam smiled, grateful, and I couldn't help but lean down and kiss him. He looked so beautiful, so trusting. I had to give him back that care, let him know I appreciated this moment.

As my tongue explored Sam's mouth, I slowly moved my hips, forward and back, letting my slacks slide against his lube-covered butt cheeks. There was a dark, wet ring forming on the fabric where it met Sam's body, so I opened the top button and let them fall down my thick thighs. I then lifted my undershirt so I could see my abs and hips as they pressed into Sam's ass.

"Harder," he whispered. "Please, sir."

I pushed back into him, faster and faster, then plunged in deep—balls to butt—and Sam's eyes shot open in surprised ecstasy. He grabbed one of my dress shoes and buried his nose and mouth in it, inhaling like it was a bottle of poppers. I increased my speed, loving the tight grip he held onto my dick, pounding into his ass, trying to focus so that I didn't cum before he did. I wanted him to shoot first, to know that I'd made him lose control before I'd chosen to finish.

His moans started instantly, rising in a high pitch from the base of his chest. He dropped the shoe, and I cupped his head with my gloved hand. Sam's eyes shot back to mine. Then they weakened slightly, like he was afraid to disappoint me. So I nodded: *You can cum now.*

With an ecstatic moan he let his juice fly, up onto my chin and then splattering back down onto his own stomach.

As he shot, I pulled my dick out, yanked the rubber off, and threw the wet wrap onto Sam's bare pec.

"Let me swallow your seed," Sam begged as cum still oozed from his piss slit. And, without waiting for permission he turned his body around so that he was on all fours, his mouth perched and ready. I let my cum fly, first hitting his chin and then going straight into his mouth. He closed his eyes but opened his mouth wider to catch it all, until he finally pressed his lips onto my sensitive head.

I tried not to shriek from my sensitivity; I needed to stay strong until every last bit of me had been drained dry.

Finally, Sam fell back and I landed on the couch next to him.

"That was ... Wow!" Sam couldn't complete his sentence, and instead started laughing.

"Just what the doctor ordered," I said, kissing his cum-covered lips.

MY NIGHT OF WILD SEX WITH WILTON PARMENTER

T. Hitman

I. Opening Teaser

One cavalry field uniform—the mounted force of the United States Army—circa 1860s. Stetson cavalry hat, with the X-insignia of crossed swords pinned above the brim. Yellow neckerchief. Shoulder stripes, with buttons down both sides of the chest on shirt. Matching yellow stripes running outer legs of pants, waist size thirty-two.

Underneath, red combination underwear. Military boots, shiny black—size twelve in my imagination, though likely tens or possibly elevens in the reality that was. Gray wool boot socks. Gun belt with scabbard for ceremonial cutlass sword.

Put together on the actor whose wiry, athletic body those clothes loved, and the result quickened my pulse, made drawing breath difficult. Body heat rose. My imagination wandered. Heavenly distraction.

It was all about that fucking uniform.

II. Theme Song

Before reality TV, the Internet—hell, even before VHS tapes—there existed a world where entertainment was delivered from writers who wrote actual stories, and actors who actually acted. Much of what came out of that era was, admittedly, cheeseball. But it was also wonderful and unforgettable, poetry projected across the black and white screen of a snowy television set hooked up to rabbit ears. When that antenna received its signal clearly, you smiled and thanked the heavens. When it didn't, you fussed and fidgeted, played with the ears, aimed them every which way, and sometimes flew into a rage because your show was coming on. Didn't matter that it was a rerun originally broadcast the same year you were born. There were fewer channels— only a handful—but the landscape then was a creative wonderland populated by westerns, crime dramas, and creature features, not the blabbering wasteland of the medium today.

As a young male secretly questioning his sexuality from the earliest age, I developed crushes on puppy dog-eyed John Gage, the hunky paramedic on *Emergency!,* and the smolderingly-handsome Officer Jim Reed from *Adam-12,* whose dispatcher in every episode urged him to *"See the man."* I saw the man, too—especially in my fantasies.

I experienced intense romantic feelings for Lurch, the towering, macho zombie dressed in his crisp butler's suit as majordomo for *The Addams Family,* and got swept up in the surreal eroticism of the "Midnight Never Ends" episode of Rod Serling's *The Night Gallery,* in which a hunky guitar-playing soldier recently returned home from war finds himself hitchhiking along a road that runs in a perpetual loop, all the way to infinity.

But there was one iconic TV character that ignited my earliest yearnings more than any other: Captain Wilton Parmenter, the clumsy, klutzy commanding officer of *F Troop* who, when he wasn't getting tangled up in his saddle when dismounting a horse or tripping over his own booted feet, sent my young heart into a gallop, and inspired carnal dreams of encounters with the man in that smart cavalry uniform.

III. First Act

At forty, after two successful decades in the TV industry working below-the-line, I landed a windfall through an inheritance. After paying off the mortgage on my bungalow in the Hollywood Hills and taxes, I still had plenty left over and pondered what to do with it. I could travel, but I'd already seen enough of the world that interested me. And, through television, I'd gone to the moon and far beyond. I could sit on it, sure—though where was the fun in that?

In between assignments, while contemplating both the money and my age, I retreated into my home office and spent the better part of the week watching videos on my tablet. Old videos from an earlier time—the TV episodes from my youth that had influenced the way my life turned out. A time warp materialized around me. I was *there* and *then* again.

I watched old low-def TV shows on my high-def modern tech, and experienced a rush of arousal that left me sweaty and constantly stiff—and jerking off to images of ghosts from my past.

"Captain Parmenter," I moaned. "Oh, *Wilton* ..."

The link appeared during that wacky sum of days, when I watched episodes of *F Troop* and then dirtied them up as re-imagined triple-X gay sex romps in which Wilton Parmenter came to me in full uniform, only to have me quickly undress him.

Studio Props and Wardrobe Auction—Authentic, Original US Cavalry Uniform—

I blinked myself out of the trance long enough to follow the link. My heartbeat quickened when the photograph showed the uniform belonging to the character of Wilton Parmenter. It hammered in my ear as I absorbed the remainder of the auction's listing: *Screen-used,* meaning the uniform had been worn by the actor on set for one or more of the actual episodes; had covered his skin, absorbed his sweat, his manly scent. I struggled for air. Breathing was no longer involuntary or easy. I paced my home office, my erection metronoming with the steps, my flesh set on fire.

The listing price was outlandish, in the thousands of dollars. I didn't care. With hands shaking, I logged into the online auction site and bid. I had the money, and I *needed* that uniform—in a manner that would make zero sense to anyone else, but to me was as vital to my happiness, to my second puberty, as those classic old television shows had been to my first.

I won the auction. I paid for insurance and express shipping, and paced some more. Days later, on a bright midweek morning, a delivery van rumbled up to my bungalow. I signed for the package, hurried into my office, and somehow managed to open the box without pinching or gouging my fingers—a routine bit of slapstick employed by Wilton Parmenter over the course of two seasons and sixty-five episodes. Hand caught in cookie jar. Goes to draw pistol, accidentally pulls out umbrella. That handsome goofball, always tripping on his way up steps or over rocks or spilling to the floor, entangled in his own two-booted feet.

I opened the box and drew out the uniform. It was exquisite, the real deal. So deep was my limerence for the character, at first I didn't realize the red long underwear wasn't part of the deal. There were no uniform boots—the pants dangled drawstrings at the bottom of the legs. No authentic, pre-worn boot socks. When I pressed my nose to the crotch of the cotton-blend material, all I smelled were the chemi-

188

cals of fifty years' worth of dry cleaning, not the heady musk of a frontier soldier's meaty, sweating balls.

I hung the uniform and sat naked before it in the silent room of an otherwise empty house, lost in thoughts that grew ever deeper, darker. The intense rush of sexual energy I'd anticipated since winning the auction never materialized. Shadows pressed in around me, filling the bungalow. This wasn't a second puberty; it was a funeral. Most of my boyhood idols were dead. The survivors were old and gray.

For days, I'd acted out scenes from *F Troop* episodes in my mind. I played the role of Wrangler Jane, the hormonal blonde beard who threw herself at Wilton Parmenter from the start of the pilot episode after a well-timed sneeze leads him and other mounted soldiers charging into a decisive Civil War battle, thus securing his command of Fort Courage, Kansas, and his troop of military misfits.

There were others who tried to get into Wilton's pants, each clearly seeing the same magnetic—albeit klutzy—he-man in uniform as I. Among them, a libidinous Julie Newmar in the episode "Yellow Bird," and a geisha in "From Karate with Love" who strips the captain out of his boots, puts him in sandals and a man's kimono, and then fawns over his every desire. I played all of those women in my fantasies, only in progressively filthier versions of the plotlines. I even didn't mind when the writers and producers of the show dressed him in a man's nightshirt and one of those ridiculous caps with a tassel—in mine, those stitches of clothing had a tendency to rapidly vanish anyway.

But that uniform was always part of the fun, and had imprinted upon my psyche from the start. Now, the same authentic uniform—*his* uniform—hung flat and two-dimensional before me.

The uniform had made the character, the man. It struck me that in order to fulfill this particular highlight of my bucket list—a *Fuck-*

it list, really—the reverse also held true. I'd need that uniform to be filled—otherwise it would always appear flaccid, and what had been would forever haunt me with what might have.

The talented actor who'd played Wilton Parmenter was well past wearing the uniform and performing the hilarious and sexy pratfalls that helped define the character. Still, after twenty years in the business, I knew plenty of casting agents, so I set out to find the man of my dreams, the man who would fill that uniform.

I started my search for a new Wilton Parmenter.

IV. Second Act

I was between jobs, had plenty of money, and understood that I was under the influence of a growing obsession that couldn't be satisfied by doing things halfway or half-assed. It was all or nothing. I'd either have it all, or I'd spend the rest of my life feeling … nothing.

I hired an unemployed set designer I'd worked with and turned him loose in my bedroom, which was the biggest appropriate space in the bungalow.

"Exactly the same?" he asked.

"Make it close enough that I forget it's a standing set and I believe the shit's real."

"I'll do my best."

"You'd better," I said.

A week later, the room transformed through the addition of an antique writing desk with a green blotter, books, and plenty of clutter on top. Salmon-pink curtains dressed fake windows. A cutlass in a scabbard dangled from a wall sconce. Chairs with tufted cushions sat before a fireplace of fake fieldstone. The antlers of a big buck hung on a wall. Even the rug matched the original enough that I was sold.

I finished personalizing the space with a set of shiny military boots, size twelve, and a pair of gray wool boot socks.

I entered the set. It was Captain Parmenter's headquarters at Fort Courage, a place I'd traveled to often enough through the TV and my dreams to recognize as a second home. My dick thickened in my jeans as the set builder pointed out this aspect of his design work or that. I reached down and adjusted my package and winced at the eruption of stars only my eyes could see.

"Yes, it's good," I said. "In fact, it's fairly fucking great. Only missing one thing."

"What's that?" he asked.

I didn't answer, paid him the balance for his services and, once alone, crawled into Captain Parmenter's bed in that far corner behind the drapes and jerked my stiff dick to climax. *Soon,* I promised myself.

My casting agent asked me about details such as waist size, height, and hair color. But when he pressed me on other specifics, I was forced to divulge the truth.

"He needs to have hair on his chest—just like in the first season episode when Captain Parmenter strips off his uniform shirt for an exam by the field medic," I confessed. "He'll need hairy arms, too, like the original Wilton Parmenter. The captain didn't show a lot of skin on the show, but those arms ... and *hands!* They prickled with dark, manly fur, especially around the wrists."

In Episode 1-27, "Don't Ever Speak to Me Again," Captain Parmenter suffered a run-in with that set of decorative buck antlers and tore off the top leg of his uniform pants, almost to the crotch. The scene, which I'd watched and rewound dozens of times on my tablet, revealed two provocative details: the first being that, for at least this particular show, my paramour had gone commando. The other—

"Hairy legs, like arms, are a must," I said.

My associate drew in an audible breath and let it sail just as loudly. "So am I to assume this casting is for an *adult* production?"

"With an audience of one."

"Understood. Listen, I have this actor in mind that might work. The right eye color and body type—though his feet are fairly big."

"Big feet works. Hair color?"

"Chestnut. Very athletic. You'll love the guy's ass—one of those perfect squares of muscle, like the original. He can pull off the goofy shit. I'm sending over his headshot."

"And he knows the kind of role he'll be playing?"

"He's hungry. Did some amateur jerk-off stuff for a gay Web site to pay his rent. Name's Ben Kerry. Oh, and he's good at voices. Check your e-mail."

A new message waited. I opened the file—and there was a photo of Ben Kerry. He was cute. Better than that, handsome, yes—an attractive young man with a bit of trendy facial hair. A modern scruffster, he grew sexier with the seconds. But he wasn't Wilton Parmenter.

"You there?" asked the voice over the phone.

"Yeah."

"What do you think?"

"I think you should keep looking."

A restless, freak rain hammered the Greater Los Angeles area and deepened the strange malaise that refused to release me from its grip. A dark day unfolded. I had work looming for pilot season, and my very own ghost town, built within the walls of my house.

I woke, jerked off in Wilton Parmenter's unoccupied bed, and was pondering another day at home in the company of secret phantoms when the doorbell chimed. I wasn't expecting anyone and, at first, wondered if I'd imagined the sound. The boundaries of reality and fantasy had blurred in recent weeks, making it difficult to tell one from the other.

I approached the front door, my heart in a gallop for reasons I couldn't define. Getting there seemed to take longer than the actual few seconds. I turned the knob and choked down a dry swallow. The door opened. A man stood on the stoop, framed by the storm. The downpour had bled all color from the new day, transforming the world into a live black and white TV episode.

He was your typical Hollywood hunk—a handsome, unshaved face and toned body clad in jeans, sneakers, and white T-shirt under a military jacket. A backpack hung off his shoulder. Maybe he was living out of it. Seeing him unleashed equal parts confusion and excitement.

"Yes?" I asked.

He fixed me with a serious look. "I hear you need a captain to run your fort."

"Huh?"

Then his expression lightened, and a smile emerged from all that facial scruff. Part of the glacier that had formed inside me melted. On my next shallow sip of breath, I drank in the fragrance of spring rain and something else. *Him.* The clean smell of his skin and sweat teased my senses.

"My name's Ben Kerry," the young man said, offering his hand. I noticed his wrist was covered in dark fur. "And I think you should give me a shot at the role of Wilton Parmenter."

Recognition dawned. "You're the actor."

"Guilty."

A feeling of paranoia crept over my flesh. "Come on," I said, and waved him into the house. I was sure that half of Hollywood was gawking at us and knew my private business.

The actor started into my bungalow. Halfway across the foyer rug, his big feet tangled and he pitched forward, straight into my arms. The man's scent filled my next gasp for air, so wonderfully seductive, his body warm and muscular against mine.

It didn't matter whether his tripping feet routine was accidental or staged. As he picked himself up and straightened, a goofy look spread across his mouth. My insides ignited. My next breath hitched in my throat.

"*Wilton*," I said.

He saluted me, and I knew he was the one.

I resisted the temptation to ask him anything regarding his own personal backstory. Just the necessary questions: How he found where I lived, how conversant he was with the material I wanted him to perform, and how far he was willing to go.

"Your casting agent believed I was your man," he said through the open bathroom door. The sound of running water played in counterpoint to his answer. His voice, I was thrilled to hear, exuded inflections reminiscent of his predecessor's. "He figured it was up to me to convince you, so here I am."

I listened with my eyes half-shut, my heart and cock both sold on him.

"And I didn't just study the part. I am Wilton Parmenter."

The water shut off. He strutted out of the bathroom, dabbing at his freshly shaved face with a towel.

I absorbed the fullness of the image he projected: his naked torso, hairy in all the right places, from chest to the treasure trail that cut him down the middle of ripped abdominal muscles; the Cavalry uniform pants that fit him to perfection, as though made for him and only him; big, bare feet, those draw strings dangling over warm skin, size twelves.

"What do you think so far, Wrangler?" he asked.

For a wondrous instant, I wasn't standing in my bungalow in the Hollywood Hills, a man in his forties haunted by unrequited lust for a beloved TV show character. I was part of the frontier landscape, living out in reality my greatest sexual fantasy.

194

I indulged in the widest of smiles and drank in a sip of air, smelling the shaving cream and the heady male smell of him.

"I think, my dashing captain, that you should answer the last of my questions."

"You mean about how far I'm willing to go?" Wilton countered.

He tossed the towel over his shoulder, real cool. I stole a glance at the dense nest of dark fur beneath his arm.

"I'm willing to go—" he started, and folded his arms. An instant later, those big feet attempted to do the same, crossing at the ankles, but slipped over the drawstrings. He reached for me, and down we both went. We landed in a tangle of limbs, with him on top of me.

"Wilton!" I gasped.

"All the way," he said after that bit of slapstick concluded.

And then he kissed me.

I walked into Captain Parmenter's headquarters. Wilton sat at his desk, writing an official communiqué with a feathery goose quill pen dipped in ink.

He glanced up, smiled. "Aah, Wrangler."

"Hello, Wilton," I said, and glided around the desk.

I pecked a kiss to his cheek. Wilton waved me away with the pen's outrageous feather.

"Now, Wrangler, we can't risk letting the men see us engaged in romantic hanky-panky."

"Oh, *Wilton Parmenter*," I whined. "It's time for you to stop working and focus on me."

He drew down the pen. The feather jammed under his nose, tickling his nostrils, and Wilton performed one of those sexy goofball shticks—face drawing back, torso following, gravity then tipping the chair beneath his butt backwards. Big feet in shiny new uniform boots flew up into the air.

I grabbed Wilton by his ankles and hauled him back down. Red-faced, Wilton flashed one of his trademark grimaces.

"Why thank you, Wrangler. I owe you one."

"You do?" I said.

Wilton's embarrassment deepened. "Now, Wrangler, you've got that devilish look in your eye …"

"And a bone in my pants. For you, my love."

I dropped to my knees between Wilton's legs.

"Wrangler!" Wilton protested.

Wasting no more time, I lifted the captain's right foot and worked off his boot. The narcotic mixture of new leather and newer sweat instantly seduced my olfactory senses. I dropped the boot, moved onto the left, baring the heavy gray wool sock beneath. I then raised his foot to my nose and stole a deep sniff off the damp underside of his toes.

"Wrangler, my feet again?" Wilton griped. "I've been sweating in those boots all day."

I smiled and sucked in another breath. My cock pulsed. My mind raced. "I know."

"But … *feet?*"

"Your feet," I said.

Reaching higher, I tugged down his boot socks, recording the scrape of his leg hair beneath my fingertips. The sock pulled free. My heartbeats quickened. For a soldier, an athlete, his feet were magnificent—big, not yet trashed by hard work and harder living, the toes long, sexy, and begging for my tongue.

I licked a series of figure eights around his toes. The captain giggled and flinched in his chair.

"Wrangler, that tickles!"

I inhaled the warm, buttery stink of his sweat, moved over to his other foot, and repeated the process. Wilton chuckled, squirmed.

"You like that?" I teased.

Wilton composed himself. "No," he huffed.

I caressed the hairy base of his calf. A glance at the tented crotch of his uniform pants confirmed my suspicion. "Liar. Your dick says otherwise."

"OK, now that's enough fooling around for now," he said. "What if Sergeant O'Rourke or Corporal Agarn were to walk in on us, or if my personal assistant Private Dobbs or Trooper Duffy saw you down there, doing—"

"It's just you and me, Wilton."

I reached higher and groped his balls. Wilton jumped up from the chair and onto those sexy bare feet. "Alone?"

"Yes, and that means there's nothing to keep us from having a night of wild sex together."

Wilton danced in place. "Sex? *Sex!*"

He pulled me off my knees and clumsily danced me away from the desk and toward his bed. Lips crushed together. My hands grabbed at Wilton's firm butt muscles and harder dick. We tumbled onto the mattress, and clothes came off along with the last of our inhibitions.

"Well, Wrangler, here I am, all yours," Wilton said.

He reclined on the bed, completely naked now, with his arms tucked behind his neck and the dopiest grin on his face, the image of a man who is about to receive the best blow job in the history of the world. I'd waited too long for this moment and didn't plan to disappoint him.

"I suppose Fort Courage can get along just fine without me while you suck my cock," he said.

I lowered between those magnificent legs. "Your cock—and one or two other body parts."

I started with Wilton's balls. He sported a decent set in a loose, furry sac. I ran my nose over his nuts the same way I had his toes, breathing in a real man's musky stink. I sucked the left between my lips, spit it out, and then drew in the other. Wilton moaned. For a second or so, he wasn't my beloved Captain Parmenter but a broke, horny actor named Ben Kerry.

"Yeah, just like that. Keep it up, Wrangler," he said, making one of those comical but also sexy facial twitches. The flicker of doubt evaporated.

I sucked both of his nuts at the same time, an action that conjured fresh sweat across his torso and made his toes curl. His cock, long and lean, matching the rest of his physique, pulsed under its own energy. My next instinct was to go higher. Instead, I licked my way under his balls, over the musky patch of fur-covered skin between his stones and asshole. I'd lusted after that butt for most of my life and here it was, mine.

"What—?" he sputtered.

My face dropped. I spread his legs, eased his butt higher, and bared the furry knot at the center of his muscled cheeks.

"Oh," said Wilton.

And, long last, I licked my way to his asshole. There, while tonguing at his pucker, I hummed the theme song to *F Troop,* and feasted.

"You know," he somehow managed, still in voice, in character. "A man could really get used to this."

Back up, I tugged on his nuts with one hand, gripped the root of his dick with the other, and squeezed. Wilton's erection jumped off his hairy six-pack, where it had leaked a puddle of clear goo, and into my waiting mouth.

"*Yes,*" he growled. "Oh, fuck!"

It didn't matter that Ben Kerry slipped out of character, because he was Wilton, *my* Wilton. I sucked his cock, pulled on his nuts. Sweat flowed. Pre-cum, too. The temperature in the room skyrocketed. Boundaries blurred. A million thoughts and memories raced through my gray matter—lust and love, premieres and cancellations, the past and the future.

"Wrangler, *fuck—here it comes!*"

He squirted a gamy blast of the batter from his nuts over my taste buds.

V. Epilogue

He bent me over, holding me about the waist with one arm, and slipped in. Wilton's sweaty weight pressed down on my spine. He exhaled a warm breath rich with the scent from my well-eaten asshole, gripped my dick with his other hand, and entered me fully. Only his nuts kept him from going even deeper.

"I was thinking," he sighed. "This … this has been great fucking fun."

I leaned against his cheek. "It sure has."

"So … if you want, we could do it again."

He eased his hips back, and I tracked the retreat of his slender cock, inch by wonderful inch. When only the head was still lodged inside my asshole, he thrust back in, and both my body and my soul ignited with electrical current.

"Yeah?" I groaned.

"You've already got this standing set, which we know is the biggest expense in any production. And there are—what?—another sixty-four episodes we could act out."

Wilton drew back and then slammed into me. A breathless expletive flew from my lips.

"And, fuck, there are so many other classic TV shows we could move onto after that, if you want."

If I wanted?

With his cock still buried deep inside me, I rolled over. Face to face, I gazed up at his perspiration-soaked handsomeness. I cupped his cheek and pulled him down for another kiss.

"Yes, my love," I sighed after our mouths parted.

And then my Wilton fucked me.

About the Editor and Authors

Born and raised in Normal, Illinois, WINSTON GIESEKE began
writing short stories and plays at a young age to escape the banality
of a healthy Midwestern upbringing. He relocated to Los Angeles at
eighteen and received a degree in Screenwriting from California State
University, Northridge, three years later. Kickstarting his career as
a television writer, he penned episodes for shows like *Wildfire* and
Hollywood Off-Ramp as well as the made-for-cable movie *Romantic
Comedy 101*, which starred Tom Arnold and Joey Lawrence. While
living in Los Angeles, he composed tantalizing copy for various adult
entertainment companies (including Penthouse.com and Napali
Video, home of "big boobs and catfights") and served as editor in
chief of both *Men* and *Freshmen* magazines before honing his jour-
nalistic skills as managing editor of *The Advocate*. An award-seeking
vocalist whose "rich voice harkens back to vintage Hollywood croon-
ers" (Gay.net), his "saucy yet heartfelt" debut album, *On the Edge*,
which "takes classic material, turns it upside down, and then spits it
out with panache" (*Frontiers*), was released in 2012. He now resides
in Berlin, an experience he shamelessly exploits at ExpatsInBerlin.
us, and is the editor of the anthologies *Indecent Exposures*, *Daddy
Knows Best*, *Straight No More*, *Blowing Off Class*, *Whipping Boys*, *Until
the Sun Rises*, and the 2014 Lambda Literary Award finalist *Team
Players*.

DAVID APRYS is a formerly innocent ex-altar boy. Originally from the Midwest, he's lived in southern California, London, and the Deep South. He now makes his home near the Chesapeake Bay. An unrepentant hedonist and keen observer of people, he's worn the hats of investigator, freelance magazine writer, and actor in his varied professional life. The author of several erotic stories published in Bruno Gmünder anthologies, he's currently hard at work on his first novel, *Changeling*.

A corporate writer by profession, RUSSELL CLARK has been writing Web sites, blogs, and brochures for years. He's happy, finally, to be writing about something he enjoys. His entire life has been spent in Southern California, where he shares his home with his dog and occasional overnight guests (usually one at a time).

LANDON DIXON's writing credits include stories in the magazines *Men, Freshmen, [2], Mandate, Torso*, and *Honcho*; stories in the anthologies *Straight? Volume 2, Friction 7, Unzipped, Wild Boys, Bad Boys, Black Dungeon Masters, Boys in Bed, Sex on the Mat, Lust in Time, Pay For Play, The Spy Who Laid Me, Latin Lovers, Indecent Exposures, Daddy Knows Best, Straight No More, Team Players, Ultimate Gay Erotica 2005/2007/2008*, and *Best Gay Erotica 2009/2014*; and the short story collections *Hot Tales of Gay Lust 1, 2*, and *3*.

MIKE HICKS is the pseudonym of a writer and editor whose fiction has appeared in the magazines *Men, Freshmen, [2], Inches, Honcho, Unzipped, Torso, Playguy*, and *Mandate*, and on the Web site of the graphic artist Patrick Fillion, where he chronicled the interplanetary erotic adventures of the characters Camili-Cat and Naked Justice. He lives with his partner in Boston, Massachusetts.

T. HITMAN is the nom de porn of a professional writer whose short fiction appeared in *Men*, *Freshmen*, and *Torso*, among others. For five years, he also wrote the *Unzipped* Web review column and contributed hundreds of interviews and feature articles on some of the hottest men in the gay porn industry.

BRETT LOCKHARD is a writer who lives in New York City with a bunch of succulents.

GREGORY L. NORRIS lives and writes in the outer limits of New Hampshire. He once worked as a screenwriter on two episodes of Paramount's *Star Trek: Voyager* and is the author of the handbook to all things Sunnydale, *The Q Guide to Buffy the Vampire Slayer*. Norris writes regularly for various national magazines and fiction anthologies, and is a judge on 2012's Lambda Awards. Visit him online at www.gregorylnorris.blogspot.com.

Before FRANCO DIMASO became a photographer (who loves to write in his spare time) he used to fly the friendly skies. He lives and works in New York City. Allegedly.

ROB ROSEN (www.therobrosen.com), award-winning author of the novels *Sparkle: The Queerest Book You'll Ever Love*, *Divas Las Vegas*, *Hot Lava*, *Southern Fried*, *Queerwolf*, *Vamp*, and *Queens of the Apocalypse*, and editor of the anthologies *Lust in Time* and *Men of the Manor*, has had short stories featured in more than 180 anthologies.

NATTY SOLTESZ's novel *Backwoods* was a 2012 Lambda Literary Award finalist and features illustrations by Michael Kirwan. His stories have been published in magazines like *Freshmen* and *Mandate* and in anthologies like *Best Gay Erotica 2011* and *Best Gay Romance*

2010. He co-wrote the screenplay for the 2009 Joe Gage-directed porn film *Dad Takes a Fishing Trip*. He lives in Pittsburgh, Pennsylvania.

JOE THOMPSON was a longtime writer for such magazine titles as *Men*, *Freshmen*, and *Unzipped*, writing everything from fiction stories and porn star interviews to articles on fetishes and gay sex culture. He also wrote for Playboy TV, and was most recently an editor at Gay.net and Gay.com.

ROGER WILLOUGHBY has interviewed erotic film stars and written porn reviews for *Men*, *Freshmen*, or *Unzipped*. He enjoys fishing and Rock Hudson movies.

Good to the Last Drop

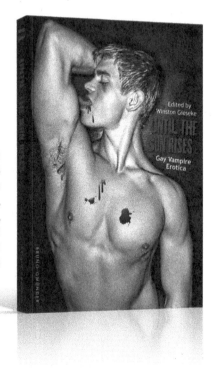

Winston Gieseke (Ed.)
UNTIL THE SUN RISES
Gay Vampire Erotica
208 pages, softcover,
13 x 19 cm, 5¼ x 7½",
978-3-86787-691-9
US$ 17.99 / £ 11.99
€ 16,95

What's so alluring about the undead? Vampires are sexy, virile, and forever young—frozen in time at their sexual peak. They have a flair for seduction, an eagerness to penetrate with more than their eyes, and an insatiable need to suck things. Their libidos and youth are rejuvenated by your blood—and to get it, they use their charm and massive strength to overpower you. What could be a bigger turn-on? Featuring explicit tales from some of gay erotica's most prolific and acclaimed authors, *Until the Sun Rises* overflows with kinky scenarios of thirsty vampires who are eager for much more than a taste of your blood.

Let's Play Master and Servant

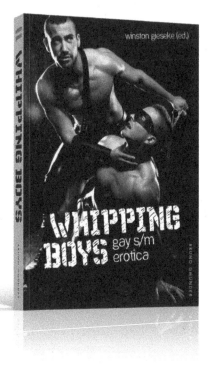

Winston Gieseke (Ed.)
WHIPPING BOYS
Gay S/M Erotica
208 pages, softcover,
13 x 19 cm, 5¼ x 7½",
978-3-86787-689-6
US$ 17.99 / £ 11.99
€ 16,95

Society has long tried to control sexual behavior with shame. But what happens when it's the shame that turns you on? In *Whipping Boys*, desire and domination take on many forms, from spanking and bondage to punishment and humiliation: A dom and his submissive share a special celebration, while a young man discovers what a naughty little pig he can be. Whether you enjoy having your hands tied behind your back or you get off putting someone in his place, this erotic anthology of extreme sex and the men who beg for it will inflict just the right amount of sting. When you fall in love, there's always a chance you'll get hurt ... when you're a whipping boy, it's guaranteed.

Gay Erotica at Its Best

Winston Gieseke (Ed.)
STRAIGHT NO MORE
Gay Erotic Stories
208 pages, softcover,
13 x 19 cm, 5¼ x 7½",
978-3-86787-607-0
US$ 17.99 / £ 11.99 / € 16,95

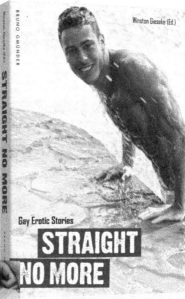

Winston Gieseke (Ed.)
BLOWING OFF CLASS
Gay College Erotica
208 pages, softcover
13 x 19 cm, 5¼ x 7½"
978-3-86787-686-5
US$ 17.99 / £ 11.99 / € 15,95

Gay Erotica at Its Best

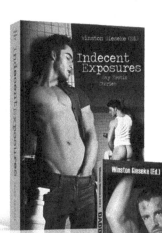

Winston Gieseke (Ed.)
INDECENT EXPOSURES
Gay Erotic Stories
192 pages, softcover,
13 x 19 cm, 5¼ x 7½",
978-3-86787-520-2
US$ 17.99 / £ 11.99 / € 16,95

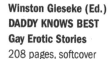

Winston Gieseke (Ed.)
DADDY KNOWS BEST
Gay Erotic Stories
208 pages, softcover
13 x 19 cm, 5¼ x 7½"
978-3-86787-590-5
US$ 17.99 / £ 11.99 / € 15,95

Winston Gieseke (Ed.)
TEAM PLAYERS
Gay Erotic Stories
208 pages, softcover
13 x 19 cm, 5¼ x 7½"
978-3-86787-609-4
US$ 17.99 / £ 11.99 / € 15,95